INSURRECTUM EX LUX LUCIS

REBELLION OF THE LIGHT

By
Frederick De Leon

www.rebellionofthelight.com

This book is a work of fiction. Places, events, and situations in this story are purely fictional. Any resemblance to actual persons, living or dead, is coincidental.

© 2004 by Frederick De Leon. All rights reserved.

No part of this book may be reproduced, stored in a retrieval system, or transmitted by any means, electronic, mechanical, photocopying, recording, or otherwise, without written permission from the author.

ISBN: 1-4107-6759-0 (e-book)
ISBN: 1-4107-6758-2 (Paperback)
ISBN: 1-4107-6757-4 (Dust Jacket)

This book is printed on acid free paper.

1st Books - rev. 01/08/04

This work is dedicated to the honor of my Father who hath made me his Son.

Prologue

Prince Leo walked the side of the mountain dressed in a long dark robe. He had the hood over his head, trying to shield his face from the rain. Many things were on his mind. For example, his mission. He had chosen it. It had not been forced upon him. His father would not and never did force anything on him. They were so alike that it almost seemed as if there was no way they could ever disagree. They thought alike and that was why he was here.

Right before him lay a huge boulder after which he would see the land. He hesitated. What would he find? What had he expected he would find? He wasn't sure. He had heard many reports of Nox, its people, their lives and of course, their king, Casus. Casus he knew personally and he thought of what it would be like to face him and stare into his eyes.

The rain was now slackening and Prince Leo thought to proceed. There was no time to sit and wonder what everything would be like when he would soon find out. He would soon be immersed in his answers.

With unnatural ease he ascended the top of the boulder and took in the sight before him. So, here lay the land of Nox. A primitive and pitiful sight. As far as he could see, the buildings were made of brick, clay or, though very few, crudely chiseled stone. But then before him lay just one city of many and this one was of somewhat meager importance. Nevertheless, there were hundreds of others just like it all over the land.

Scanning with his eyes the sight before him, Prince Leo instantly felt the pang of depression pierce his soul. He had envisioned the final battle being glorious. He had always imagined himself in that great fight releasing all the power and might within his frame. He had often smiled at the thought of going against unbelievable odds yet turning out to be the victor. But looking out at this city, he was now forced to realize that it would be nothing like that. Just as he had always suspected and dreaded. There would be no great glory to be had by him. On that day, he might not even break a sweat. These people would simply be overran. The whole thing might not even last an hour. There is no way that these people and the meager forces of Casus could stand up to the forces of his father Unus.

He thought of their own cities that were filled with mansions, walls of gold, silver and plastered pearls designed with exquisite engravings. The plentiful gardens and radiant colors of flowers, clothes and thousands of jeweled ornaments. He thought of the healthy bodies of the citizens who ate the best meats and drank the best wine everyday of their lives. He thought of how they never knew weakness or frailty of limbs but enjoyed omnipresent healing. Most of all, he replayed in his ears the laughter of the children as they ran through the luscious green fields playing with the slightest hint of worry farthest from their tender minds. They knew no fear nor sadness. Their lives were full of light and heartiness. His father insured that.

But all that was Seven Seas and Seven Mountains away. As he looked down at the weary souls going in and out of the city through its dilapidated walls, he felt a sharper pain deep down within him. He could tell that the people who lived there were beaten down, crushed and had given up hope of anything. He could feel the spirit of the place and its people as he looked down at their land, their homes and their lives.

Why? Why did things have to be this way? Why did the children of this place not live in Lux, his land and the land of his father. Why did they not play in his fields and eat fruit from the trees there? He had heard that many of the children of Nox hardly had enough food to eat. That many of them starved and were forced to work, labor for any chance of bread. That many of them had no proper learning if any learning at all. There were children who had been abandoned by either one or the other of their parents if not both. Here in this land of Nox, he had heard that a man would have children by a woman and leave her alone to tend to them. Alone! Even babies. Babies! Unwanted! Abandoned! Babies! How could anything be so wrong? How could anyplace be so backward and absurd?

He felt the anger boiling up inside of him, making him hot in the midst of the wet and dreary weather. He looked down at his fists which were clenched tight and he felt his jaw muscles flex and tighten. All the muscles in his body were wide awake.

All this horror was Casus' doing. All of it! All lands were once under his father Unus and he was the king of all. Everywhere, no matter how far away from the seat of his throne, he ruled and there was peace and happiness. Even this present wasteland that now lay before his eyes flourished with the glories of the kingdom. There was an abundance of corn, meat, honey, milk and wine everywhere. Unus made it his duty to insure that every child had more than enough under his hand. He set forth laws that were fair and just for everyone. There was no thing as corruption or injustice. All men were to honor and respect his fellow. All men were to work, not labor, but work at his trade and talents and all men thereby profited appropriately so as to insure life and pleasure.

But Casus had to ruin everything. His high seat of honor in the kingdom was not enough. He had to have everything for himself. He had to be the king. He had to rule all lands himself. Hadn't he, Prince Leo, warned his father that Casus had busied himself with causing dissent amongst the other rulers? Didn't he warn his father of what would happen if Casus was allowed to continue his diabolical affairs? But his father had always remained silent on the matter. He never did say or do anything. Whenever Leo broached the subject of what was going on within the kingdom, he would always just turn and walk away . The stench of it had been driving Prince Leo quite beside himself and so it was difficult for him to understand why his father was reacting or rather, not reacting, the way that he was. He knew that it was not because Unus was getting weak or was afraid. Prince Leo shared Unus' strength and energy and the force of it was not diminished in the slightest.

If it were, he, Leo would have felt it and there could be no way for Unus to disguise it from him. They were both connected at a center core of life force, one Intimus Essentia. So then, what was the problem? Why was his father allowing this?

Then came that dreadful morning when magnificent Sedes, the crown city and center of the kingdom, was stormed. Casus and his fellow seditionist led a fierce attack from within the city. They wrecked havoc everywhere and turned the city up side down. They destroyed tapestries, hurled down statues of pearl, ivory, marble and bronze and smashed beautifully crafted stain glass windows. They set fire to the city and began to destroy buildings on their way to the palace. He, Leo, had sent as many men as he could to stop the traitor and his co-hordes but had decided, himself, to stand guard at the doors of King Unus' chambers. He was soon appalled to find out that their forces had been beat back by Casus' numerous and determined hordes. Only days before he had cautioned Unus to call back many of the troops that were loyal from all over Lux to defend Sedes should anything happen. To his utter dismay, his father sent more than half of the city's permanent troops as far away from the city as possible! Now they were outnumbered and it wasn't long till he could hear Casus and his forces crossing the River Vivere to Unus' chambers. The rage he, Leo, felt at that moment was surpassed only when he stood face to face with Casus and stared him in the eyes. He began summoning the fiercest might of his energy to obliterate them all in the most terrifying way when he heard his father's calm, but firm, voice within his head.

Step aside.

Prince Leo knew that those massive doors to Unus' chambers were still closed behind him. Those steel doors were seven miles thick, holding back his father's glory yet they always seemed on the verge of bursting. For this reason, no one had really seen King Unus save Leo. All anyone else had ever seen were faint images of Unus projected from behind those doors. He never would forget the look on Casus' face when he stepped aside. Casus knew that Prince Leo would never join his cause, so then why was he stepping aside and not fighting to protect his beloved father? Was this some trick?

But surely before Casus could think his next thought, the doors flung open with excessive force, releasing infinite light so strong that the waves of it, more powerful than all the waves of the Seven Seas, forced Casus and every one of his troops far out of Sedes and onto the shores of this land, then known as Hortulus. Casus, livid with anger, hate and unthinkable shame, vowed to strike back. But this time no longer from without, but from within. He would attack Unus' from within his own heart and cause him to bleed. He would destroy his precious people and cause them to hate him. With great cunning, Casus convinced the keepers of Hortulus to make him their own private king which, to their chagrin, they did. Thus the land was transformed from Hortulus, meaning "little garden", and that it was, to Nox, a land of starvation and want.

All this was a long, long time ago. Things have remained the same since that terrible day. Generations have both come and gone. He had heard that many of the inhabitants of Nox no longer believe the stories of the things that happened long ago or that their land was once very different from the way that it now is. He had heard that many of these people do not even believe in his existence, nor the existence of his father. There are even some who don't believe cause they've never heard. How interesting. The same disbelief applied to Casus. He, Leo, had heard reports that many of these people didn't know or believe that Casus is ruling and reigning their land behind the scenes with his hands ever on the pulse of things. To many of the people of Nox, these facts are nothing but old wives tales, fables.

Prince Leo fixed his eyes on two old people headed for the city. They must be drenched in this rain. He on the other hand wasn't because he didn't want to be. That meant that the power within him dried up the rain before it touched his skin or robe. But the couple there, they were wet. He could tell. He wondered how they would react if he were to tell them that King Unus, the Lord of All Lands, was presently preparing to march on this land and annihilate all of its rebellious inhabitants? What if he told them to leave the land of Nox and flee to the mountains and the seas to meet the king and his troops and beg safety? What if he told them that the king could be here quite suddenly and at anytime? What would they do? What would they say? Would they take his advice and leave? Would they call him an idiot and turn their backs on him? Or would they put their lives on the line to help him establish the rebellion?

Prince Leo jumped off the boulder and began his decent down the mountain side. There was only one way to find out.

THE CITY OF EGENUS

Chapter One

Though the slope was muddy, slippery and completely dangerous, Prince Leo was not afraid. He knew his balance was sure. Because of his inner force, he would never slip and fall. His thoughts were on the two elderly people in the distance headed for the city and the shelter of its meager walls. Despite the fact that they were a considerable distance from him, he could feel them shiver and sniffle, being drenched and trekking in this rain. His heart went out to them. They belonged in a warm room, before a fireplace, nice and snug, sipping hot teas or having a warm bowl of meal. But they were out in the cold rain walking to the city. This could never had been the case in Lux. Never!

With purposed and determined speed, Prince Leo was upon them in no time. His heart broke even further when he saw that they had no shoes on their feet but walked barefoot. What kind of abominable inferno was this place? Why ought this happen anywhere at anytime? So this was the rule of Casus? Misery and the lack of pity? No heart, no feeling, no emotion?

Prince Leo's thoughts were interrupted. He heard something. It was far off and in the distance but he could hear it. He stopped to listen, to concentrate and to see what was making the noise and causing the disturbance within him.

Horses. About...nine thousand horses! They were coming from the north, the west and the south.

Someone was staring at him. The old woman had stopped and was staring at him strangely. The old man, noticing she had stopped, turned to see what was the matter, and seeing that she was staring at him, also took up interest. Prince Leo at first didn't know what to do neither did he realize why he seemed to be so interesting that they would stop in the rain.... He looked down at himself. His clothes. He wasn't wet while they were drenched in the rain.

He smiled at them nervously, removing the hood from over his head. They didn't smile back.

"My name is Leo."

They said nothing in return. They simply continued to stare at him. Soon, however, the ground began to shake. Then they tore their attention away from him and began to try to figure out what was going on.

"Horses," Prince Leo said. "It's horses."

Hearing that, they immediately turned and started running for the city. Then Leo understood. It was an attack on the city. Three thousand horsemen from the north, the south and the west respectively and all at once.

Sadly, he turned his attention to the couple ahead of him, running as hard as they could. Measuring in his mind, the intensity of the sound with the rate at which the couple was running and the distance they yet had to go, he knew that even if they kept their pace ,which was impossible at their ages, they would never make it.

He remembered promising King Unus, his father that he would restrain himself and not interfere in every situation he encountered. The people of Nox had chosen their lives and they must be allowed to live their choice. The king had reminded him that Nox was a land of evil and that evil was the inheritance of its inhabitants who chose to spit in the face of his lordship. King Unus allowed the followers of Casus to kill and maim each other, starve each other and do whatever their new leader encouraged them to do. These people and their parents had chosen Casus over their rightful king and Unus wanted to give some respect to that choice. Those of these people who knew of King Unus knew for a fact that such unbecoming and atrocious behavior would be unheard of under his rule. But then he wasn't the ruler of this place now was he? And so right before Leo's eyes, a virtually defenseless city was being attacked.

Prince Leo had stopped by now. He could see the horses coming from all three directions, steadily descending upon them. The old woman ahead of him, in her haste and terror, slipped and fell into a puddle. The old man stopped to help her, beside himself with fear.

Fear. That was something Prince Leo had never really known. What did it feel like to be utterly and completely afraid? Why be afraid? Well for him, he could understand why he was never afraid? What could possibly harm him, Prince Leo, Son of King Unus? But for these feeble beings, he could imagine why they were familiar with terror, with fear. Both he and his father had sworn to protect them but they had turned their backs on that protection. Now, under the rule of Casus, they had as much protection as a chicken with its head on the chopping board before the swing of the blade.

"What are you doing here," a sinister but very familiar voice asked.

Prince Leo heard the voice in his head and instantly recognized its owner. It was a voice he hadn't heard in a very, very long time. Was he among the troops on the verge of storming this pathetic city? He scanned the three directions covered with horsemen.

No. Casus was not among them.

"Again, my prince, I ask, what are you doing here?"

The thunderous hooves of the nine thousand horses pounded the ground and shook it even more as they approached. Prince Leo could see the chunks of mud being kicked up as the cloud of horsemen descended upon them. The elderly couple and a few others still frantically racing in vain for the city.

"My lord, Prince Leo, do you not answer me," the voice calmly asked.

You address my son, Casus?

It was his father. It was King Unus' voice.

"My king," Casus could be heard replying, "I merely sought to inquire as to why I am so honored by the prince's visit. I ought to have been formally informed that I might have provided a more adequate reception for someone as esteemed as he."

Leo, he heard his father address him.

"Father?"

Remove yourself from the field.

Prince Leo looked again over at the elderly couple and a few others who were all still a good distance from the city's gates, gates which were now being hastily closed before them. They would, could, never make it in time.

"Father...."

No Leo. Not here, not now.

"Yes Leo. Not here and not now," Casus' voice tauntingly reiterated.

One of the horsemen was now five feet away from him and preparing to swing his axe at Leo's head. With one last glance at the couple ahead of him, Prince Leo slowly vanished off the field while a sharp metal blade swung at where his noble head used to be.

Chapter Two

Prince Leo watched the destruction from a distance. He saw the slaughter, carnage and pillaging. He heard the cries of the women being raped and then murdered. He felt mammoth grief overtake his soul as the tears rolled down his face. His rage burned as he saw the army gallop away, proud of themselves and cheering, leaving the already miserable city engulfed in flames. He wanted to gather them, the attackers, all together and hurl them into a burning inferno of lava and have them remain there forever without the relief of death. He wanted to rip their hearts out of their chests and squeeze the life out of it.

They are victims too.

He was on the verge of hating his father right now. He didn't want to hear his voice. He didn't want to listen to his reason, his wisdom. Prince

Leo wanted to hate. He wanted to feel boiling, scalding rage and empower himself with it.

That's not how you empower yourself. You know that. Going about things that way leads you onto a path of madness; it's a double-edged sword that will in time turn on you and destroy you.

But why father, Prince Leo asked within himself. I demand to know why. Why this way?

What's more important right now are the survivors. Go to them.

True. Why sit here asking questions to which he knew the answers when there where those who needed him, when there where those who desperately needed comfort. Even now he could feel the faint throbbing of hearts, some of them dangerously faint, but still there.

Let love empower you my son. Empower you to both destroy and to build. But let love empower you.

Prince Leo went to the burning city and entered its tossed aside and flaming gates. There where bodies everywhere. Limbs askew from bodies, severed heads of women and children, not to mention men, and it seemed that the ground had drank so much blood that it didn't want anymore. Yet in the midst of it all there was still life, hope.

Prince Leo went to a pile of bodies and pushing them aside, uncovered a frightened little girl, about the age of six. Seeing him, she immediately began to scream.

"It's okay, it's okay. They're gone now. I've come to help. Don't worry.

I won't let anyone hurt you."

Prince Leo allowed a portion of who he was to go out to her and quiet her spirit. She flung herself into his arms crying.

Trust, Leo thought to himself. Even after all this, it didn't take much for a child to trust.

Goodness, he heard Unus' voice whisper, *is a light that shines through darkness.*

The girl was still sobbing frightfully in his arms.

"Shhh. Shhh. It's alright now. No one's going to hurt you. I promise. Shhh. It's okay," Prince Leo comforted the child.

She continued to whimper however, and she had good reason. Prince Leo could tell that both her parents had been killed in the attack. Her father while trying to defend the city and his family within and her mother had been raped and then beheaded as this little girl watched helplessly from a hidden place. Now, she had no one in the world. No one.

Slowly and cautiously, people began to emerge from the ruins. Prince Leo lifted the little girl to his shoulders and began to pat her back to soothe her. He walked through the city, drawing a small crowd of curious people wondering who this stranger was and why he was there. Prince Leo found the steps of what used to be a large building and climbed the steps.

"Child, what's your name?" Leo asked the little girl on his shoulder.

"Maeror."

"Okay Maeror, I'm going to talk to these people for a little bit, okay?"

She nodded her head, never letting go of him.

Prince Leo opened his mouth to speak and it was as if it were the music of the Seven Seas descending on the people like dew from the Seven Mountains.

"I am Prince Leo of Lux, Son of King Unus, Lord of All Lands. Come to me."

There was hesitation in the crowd. But at the same time, there was power and authority in that voice such as they had never known. And their hearts were ripe.

One man stepped forward out of the crowd and approached Prince Leo. His left arm was smashed and he was holding it up with his right hand. There were tears in his eyes as he looked at Prince Leo who was also feeling within his own body the man's pain.

The little girl on his shoulder turned around to see what was happening. Prince Leo reached out his right hand toward the man's left arm. He allowed his life force to reach out and touch the man's own life force and like a current going through his arm, the smashed bones and skin began to return to perfect form.

For a moment everyone stared. They stared into space and for an instant, though they were not yet born, remembering a perfect time of a land with healing waters and brilliant light. They remembered a place of peace and crystalline happiness. They remembered something pure.

Prince Leo was rushed by the crowd of people, each person pushing forth an injured limb, slashed arm, bleeding heads and every ailment they had procured both before and during the attack. Prince Leo almost fell over with the little girl in his arms. He quietly closed his eyes, and amid the cacophony of noise, thought of his home, the land of Lux, the glorious city of Sedes and the mystical waters of Vivere. He connected his being with the immaculate existence of the place he called home and seeing before him the face of his sovereign, a wave was released from his body, touching and transforming everyone around him.

Fires were still burning all over the city, devouring homes, shops, livelihoods. Prince Leo thought that there had been enough pain and destruction for one day. He thought it was a good time for a gentle rain and instantly, warm droplets began to fall from the dark night sky.

Before him people were crying and celebrating. They had never experienced or felt what they just did. With the drops from the sky came hope and a sublime ring of peace. Prince Leo looked out at them and felt their relief, their hope and the calm after the storm. He loved them. He was glad that they were happy but was distressed that the bodies of the elderly couple he had seen earlier lay broken, mangled and slashed outside the city walls.

Chapter Three

Prince Leo woke up the next morning with Maeror sleeping beside him. He recalled she hadn't left his side the entire night before. To think that at this very hour, a day before, she had a mother and father, a home and a bed to sleep in, a somewhat stable life. A day later, she lay here on the cold, hard concrete floor clinging to a perfect stranger for safety and security. He knew she felt safe with him. The trauma of losing her parents was abated when she was in his presence. But what would happen when he had to leave? He knew he would have to stay here for a few days in this city and with these people. He would have to help these people rebuild. He would start his work here. In this city where he first saw the work of Casus against his and his father's people, this is where he would sow the seeds to corrupt the corruption and rebel against the rebellion.

But in a matter of days perhaps, it would be time for him to leave. He would have to go on to different cities and sow discord there. What would become of these people? What would become of this little girl suddenly orphaned?

Father?

No.

Then where will she live? Who will take care of her? She just yesterday lost her parents and have attached herself to me only to be left alone again? I fear for her.

Allow her to live in her world. Allow her to live her life. In the world she lives in, they all have to be strong and tackle their own very different and distinct life situations. Also don't forget, I have some of our people all over Nox. I will watch over her but you must stay focused on the larger picture. Remind the people of Nox of my Testament to them. Tell them to prepare for our arrival and to swear their loyalties to me so that when I come, I may protect those that are my own. I am going to destroy the land of Nox and restore it to its former self. I am going to turn Nox back into Hortulus, a splendid little garden of abundant fruit and cool breezes, exquisite flowers and soft meadows. A place where once again children can play and be cheerful. A place where my people can live in peace and happiness.

But father I have to understand. Why this difficult path to something beautiful? Why did you not crush Casus from the start or even allow me to liquify him and his rabble of fools with intense fires? Had it been so, this child would not be enduring such unspeakable horrors at this tender age.

In time, you will understand.

The door to the room creaked open and a man poked his head in.

"My lord?"

"Yes. I am well," Leo replied sitting up.

Prince Leo pulled himself off the uncomfortable floor. Actually his night's sleep had been horrible. He was accustomed to the ultimate comforts of the City of Sedes. His chambers in the palace were lavished with things that were better than the best anywhere, yet he had passed the night in the most crude manner.

"We have prepared you meal," the man said.

"Thank you. Your name?"

"Fortis, my lord."

"Ah, well Fortis, may I wash first?"

"Aye my lord. We have heated water for you."

"Again my thanks Fortis. To both you and your people."

"We are...your people now, my lord."

Prince Leo, somewhat startled by that statement, turned and looked at the man. Fortis' head was bowed down as he felt Prince Leo's eyes on him.

"I hope so Fortis. I sincerely hope so."

"The child, my lord?"

"Let her sleep. She's been through a lot. When she wakes, make her wash and bring her to me."

"Yes my lord."

Prince Leo went and washed himself. He was most grateful for the hot water. It both awakened and revived him. Though it was only a little comfort, he would learn to appreciate and enjoy it just as these people did. He would live with them, the way they lived and thereby be better able to relate to them and the rest of the people of Nox. He would show to as many of these people as were willing, the way to Lux so that there, they might be able to live better lives. That was his entire desire, that as many of these people as were willing, would live better. He would not force or coerce them, however. Only, as many as were willing to leave this land or assist him to help others leave, he would gather to himself and they would join him and his father. All lands would be one again soon whilst the fate of Casus, his hordes and those who loved them and followed them would be blamed on no one. They had decided to wage war against King Unus and his son and so they all together will have to bear the consequences of that decision.

He went out to find Fortis and the others. He was hungry and felt like it. Smoke still lingered over the charred pieces of wood and the destruction of the day before appeared even more obvious and unnecessary in the morning light.

"My lord."

"Fortis, so where might we have a bit to eat?"

"This way my lord."

Fortis led the way and Prince Leo followed. He was, though, uncomfortable with Fortis' formal manner. Although he deserved all the honor and respect he was being given, he wanted more to be seen as a friend. He wanted these people to love rather than fear him.

"Here my lord," Fortis said pulling a half charred chair for him at a table covered with old red cloth. There was a big bowl of meal and some fruit. A pitcher and a cup sat on the side.

"Why is there only one chair?" asked Prince Leo.

"My lord?"

"Where are the other chairs and where is everyone? Where and when are you going to eat? Have you eaten at all?"

"No. No my lord?"

"Well, where is everyone?"

"They are preparing to eat my lord."

"I would like to eat with them. Is that alright?"

"Of course my lord. As you wish."

"Leo."

"My lord?"

"Call me Leo."

"I can't my lord, forgive me."

"Well, whatever is comfortable for you. But please, help me take this food to where the rest of the people are."

"Aye my lord."

Prince Leo took the bowl of meal while Fortis took the fruit and pitcher and led the way through the ruins towards the makeshift kitchen. Before they had even reached the fires over which the meal was being cooked, they met the curving, swerving lines where the hungry and battered were hoping to have something hot in their stomachs. Prince Leo saw some people sitting around, slurping at the hot breakfast. Some were eating out of broken bowls, cups, pot and pan tops, whatever they could find that might be able to contain the measly ration without spilling it onto the ground. From the look of things, the city had also been looted. These people were left with nothing.

"Fortis?"

"Yes my lord?"

"What was the attack about? Who was it anyway that attacked you?"

"We were attacked by the city Elatus my lord."

"Elatus?"

"Yes my lord. They are south of this place."

"But you were attacked from three directions."

"They got aid from other cities my lord."

"But why did they attack you so, so viciously?"

"They are better than us my lord. Bigger and stronger. And we were unable to pay the rent...."

"Rent? Why pay rent? Rent for what?"

"For living here my lord. For about everything, really. We just pay rent. That's how its always been."

"Did they build this city?"

"No my lord."

"Did they own this land?"

"Own this land? My lord, we have lived here since the beginning of all."

"Then why do they demand rent?"

"Because they do my lord."

It didn't make sense. Only under Casus' rule, Leo thought to himself as he shook his head, confounded at what he heard. Only under Casus' rule.

"What is the name of your city Fortis?"

"It is Egenus my lord."

"Egenus," Prince Leo repeated as he paused for a while.

"I am changing the name. From now on it shall be called Spes."

They reached the heart of the kitchen and met the women in rags, grinding corn and wheat and pouring it into a boiling caldron of water. They were all shocked to see Prince Leo in their midst, obviously not eating elsewhere.

A woman came up to him slowly and with her head bowed down. Without raising her head to look at him, she asked him a question.

"Is there something wrong with your meal my lord?"

"No," Prince Leo replied. "Nothing at all. I would just like us all to eat together that's all."

The woman looked at Fortis as if expecting him to translate what she had just heard. She seemed unable to understand why he, Prince Leo, would want to eat with them.

Fortis nodded to her.

"But where will you sit my lord," the woman asked, her head still bowed down.

"I will sit where everyone sits," Prince Leo replied as he reached out his hand under her chin and lifted her head so that he could see her face and she could see his.

Prince Leo took his bowl, went to the line and pulled a boy and a girl out of the line, inviting them to eat with him. They seemed timid at first, but their growling stomachs soon got the best of them. They all three sat on the ground together and ate the bowl of meal while it was still hot. The children didn't talk much but ate heartily. These children too had lost parents in the attack.

Soon the meal was all gone and Prince Leo gave the fruit to the children who ran off. He went over to Fortis who had been helping the women.

"Fortis you do not eat?"

"Nay my lord."

Prince Leo knew why. There wasn't enough for everybody.

"Fortis, eat. There will be more than enough for all of us. Trust me. Eat friend. There is much to do."

"Yes my lord."

Fortis was a strong man but had been broken the day before. He had lost a wife and all of his five children. He was all alone. He had no idea that Prince Leo was aware of the fact that he had snuck out of the city late last night with all of their bodies and buried them outside the city walls. Prince Leo knew that this big, strong man had been brought to heart rending sobs alone in the dark, moonless night and was even now having trouble seeing hope and purpose for the future.

That is why, for Fortis, Maeror, and all the survivors of the terrible day before, Prince Leo would make sure that there would be a bright and shining sun high up in their dark sky.

Maeror ran to him and jumped into his arms. Prince Leo picked her up and swung her around. She screamed with laughter and he put her down.

"Have you eaten?" he asked her.

"No. Not yet."

"Well, go on and get something to eat."

"Okay."

A young lady came and took Maeror away. Fortis came up to him.

"My lord, we have good news. We have found twenty more bags of corn and six bags of wheat that the soldiers didn't see or overlooked! There will be more than enough for everybody, but for today that is."

"Fortis," Prince Leo spoke softly while staring into space. "How many people survived?"

"Three hundred," Fortis replied with his head bowed and his mood suddenly changing. He was obviously struggling with his emotions.

"Out of how many," Prince Leo asked.

"Twenty-two thousand."

A tear streaked down the face of Fortis. Prince Leo put his hand on his shoulder.

"There is coming a brighter day friend, in spite of your loss."

"There can never be," Fortis replied, anger evident in his voice.

"Look at me Fortis."

Fortis raised his head and looked Prince Leo in the eyes.

"There shall be."

"If you say my lord," Fortis tried to look away.

"I do say! Call the people. I will speak to them. Men, women and children."

"Aye my lord."

"How many men do we have?"

"Seventy."

"Of the three hundred?"

"Yes my lord."

"The rest women and children?"

"Aye."

"Starting now, every male child shall be a man and every female child shall be a woman. Bring them to me Fortis. There is much to do."

Chapter Four

"A great and terrible horde overtook you yesterday and we all still feel the pain of it. You because you were the receivers of the evil and I because I beheld all of it. However, wallowing in the pits of sorrow and despair shall aright nothing. Today, the present, is new. Today calls upon us all to answer its call and make all things new. You have been beaten but not vanquished for life is yet within you. So is hope. I pledge myself to you all to help you rebuild your homes, your lives. I will lead you into a brighter day than you have ever known. I will show you the light of my land and will establish your strength. This city shall no longer be called Egenus, but I now name it Spes. I am here to resurrect you from these ashes and to give to you glory you have never known before.

"I have left my land, the glorious land of Lux, to come here, to your land of Nox, to show you all the light of King Unus, Lord and Master of All Lands. He, my father, designs that you all prosper in health and spirit. Under his rule, no such atrocity such as that of yesterday could ever happen. Tears will be functions of joy rather than pain. I know you all have heard of the Testament of King Unus sent here a long, long time ago. I urge you to both hallow and keep its oath for even now the mighty forces of Lux stomp impatiently on the horizon to trample Nox and all its people who reject the Standard of Light. For too long evil has reigned o'er Nox and its people, grinding you to dust and breaking your spirits. I say let it end here and now and let that end begin with you. Take oath to the One King, Unus and I swear to you that you shall never again see a setting sun!"

There came a loud roar which started with some of the men and spread through all the people. Tears streamed from eyes and passion ignited hearts. There was a current in the air as Prince Leo fed off of their fervor and sincerity.

Fortis stepped forward. His face wet with the tears of his eyes.

"I swear oath to the king, King Unus of Lux, Master of All Lands. Till death I will keep the Testament of the King and shall hold high the Standard of Light in this very land."

Maeror ran to Prince Leo and he picked her up. One by one they continued to swear oath to the king and take his Testament.

"What is it exactly do you think you are doing?"

Prince Leo recognized the voice and smiled with hate.

What do you think I'm doing, Prince Leo replied without parting his lips. I am going to give you a taste of your own drug. I will have your loyal subjects rebelling against their Lord Casus and after I have successfully planted the seeds of rebellion in this little kingdom of yours, I will take you up on your offer of hospitality and inspect your pathetic pit of a palace before I return to Lux, gather my forces and come knocking once more on your front door to finally smash you to bits. That's what I'm doing, Casus.

"You had better return to Lux and your beloved father while I still let you!"

Oh my dear Casus, Prince Leo shot back with all the sarcasm he could muster, that would not be a threat would it? Do you forget that had my father not held me back so long ago, we would not presently be having this discussion? Do you forget your place? You and your band of jesters owe me your very existence.

"And may I remind you, dear prince, that it was I and my 'band of jesters' that stormed your beloved City of Sedes and destroyed it and have these miserable and disgusting creatures here in Nox by the throat? What if I forget myself and squeeze, prince? What happens then? You can do nothing but sit, cry and be broken hearted. You and your detestable father. So if you don't want me to break that fragile heart of yours, I suggest you run back to your daddy, to Lux!"

You forget yourself Casus. Your lengthy time away has dulled your thinking. I believe that you have forgotten a lot of things and I shall be more than happy...to remind you.

"Fortis," Prince Leo called him aside amidst the roaring crowd drunk

Frederick De Leon

with excitement.

"Yes my lord."

"Prepare the people," with a stern face and fierce brow, Prince Leo stared at the people. "There is going to be another attack on the city come nightfall."

Chapter Five

Prince Leo sat alone in the dark room, the same room he had slept in the night before. Had Casus completely lost his mind? He, Leo, thought that he had once before when he led the attack on his father, Unus, but his tone today had been somewhat surprising. He dared now to threaten the Prince of Lux? No one had ever dreamed to dare but here was Casus openly defying him. This shocked than angered him. No one had ever threatened he Leo before. Had Casus tapped into some hidden, secret power that could match his own or that of his father? That would be the only sensible explanation for his behavior. Any other would be lunacy. But then again, what power could there be that could be mightier than the force of his father's right hand? Besides, it wasn't like Casus hadn't defied them before.

Defend the city.

I shall father.

Defend only the city. Only this city. Tonight.

Why do you speak like that? What do you mean by saying only the city?

You will see.

I suppose. Will I be honored by King Casus' presence tonight?

You ought to know he won't appear.

His boldness surprises me. Let me torture him when I meet him. Put him in his proper place.

No. Let's stick to the scheduled plan. Then you can do whatever you choose to.

Father?

Yes.

I will protect these people but what of the others in this kingdom. Casus will destroy many simply out of spite or to vent his rage.

He will.

What do I do about that?

Stick to the plan. No matter what he does. He is only trying to dissuade you from carrying out your mission. Though he doesn't know all that it entails, he's smart enough to know that it can't be good for him or his cause. What we have devised is excellent and will frustrate him far more than anything else we could do at this juncture.

But father, the people. The innocents he will sacrifice in order to attempt to stop us. What of them?

Well, there is no harm that Casus can do that we can't undo. You don't worry about that. Just stick to the plan.

I will. I will.

When Prince Leo stepped outside it was dark. The sun had been high and shining as bright as it possibly could in Nox when he retreated into his bare concrete room to gather and prepare himself. The crowd had been loud, jovial, excited and hopeful. Now it was quiet, dark and hardly anyone was around. Only, there was a young lad standing outside his door.

"How are you," Prince Leo asked the boy.

"I'm well my lord."

"What's your name?"

"Promptus my lord."

"Where is everyone Promptus?"

"I don't know my lord. Fortis told me to stand here until you came out and then to get him. Shall I?"

"Yes."

Then Prince Leo changed his mind.

"No. Take me to him."

The young man leading the way, Prince Leo and Promptus walked through the ruined city. The night air was cool with a lingering stench of smoke, and death. One could hardly see anything in the darkness. For the first time, Prince Leo was actually feeling how deserted the city was. He could tell that a lot of work had been done during the day, burying the dead, but more would have to be done the next day. All this death and dying was beginning to get to him. But he couldn't worry about that right now. He had a job to do. He was on a mission that he had to accomplish. He could not allow anything to deter or distract him.

Prince Leo looked at the young man ahead of him. Did he know what was going on around him? How much of it did he actually understand?

"Promptus," Prince Leo asked him, "are you aware that there is going to be an attack on the city tonight?"

"Yes my lord. Fortis told us after you had left," he replied over his shoulder without turning around.

"Aren't you afraid?"

"No my lord. I lost my uncle, aunt, cousins and only sister in the attack yesterday. Today I took oath to King Unus and took his Testament. I am not afraid."

"Even if you are to die tonight?" Prince Leo persisted.

"I have nothing my lord. All I now have is life and I have taken oath. I am not afraid."

Prince Leo knew the lad was serious and meant every word he said. He was impressed.

"Well, my young friend, you have nothing to fear from this night."

They arrived to where Fortis had told Promptus he would be, by the front gate of the city or what had once been the front gate of the city. An inviting gap now replaced the huge iron and wooden gate. Fortis was standing there with two other men. They were all covered in whatever pieces of armor they could find, coat of mail and armed with swords, spears and shields. Leo smiled.

Fortis, seeing him, immediately took Prince Leo aside.

"My lord, it's not at all good. When news of the many troops marching against us hit the city, the people began to despair. Mighty men from Despero and Dubito led by men from Scelus will be here any time soon. The men from Scelus especially strike fear into the people my lord. The people of Scelus are filled with wickedness. They are renown for their cruel and terrible tortures."

Prince Leo expected this. This was Casus' tactic and an effective one it was.

"There is more my lord. Some of the people have fled the city."

Prince Leo had suspected this too. That was why his father had not said to protect the people of the city, but to protect the city. Had he said to protect the people of the city, he would have been able to protect both those who had fled and those who remained. King Unus had known that this would happen. Now, he, Leo, could only protect those who had stayed with him. A sad course of events.

"How many have left us Fortis?"

"One hundred thirteen men, women and children."

A tear lid down Prince Leo's face.

"My lord. Fortis," Promptus said almost in a whisper and cautiously approaching them. "The city is surrounded."

Prince Leo was heartbroken. Why had the people not trusted? Why had they fallen so soon and wavered after swearing oath? Why had they so much fear and distrust? Did they think him weak? He, the son of King Unus, weak and unable to protect them, defend them? Was he incompetent?!

Anger and rage began to choke him. He had been defied and insulted.

He would have to teach Nox a lesson, a very memorable one.

"Any sign of those that had left the city?"Prince Leo asked.

Promptus shifted his feet nervously.

"What boy! Speak!" Prince Leo demanded.

The boy, trembling, managed to speak.

"Some heads on the end of spears."

Prince Leo felt a deadly furor rumbling deep down within him, getting stronger and intensifying till it overtook his entire body. His feet and hands began to tremble terrifying those standing around him. He suddenly threw his head back and let out a bloodcurdling roar. The ground beneath him began to shake. Fortis and Promptus seeing this ran away from Prince Leo, petrified and not knowing what to think of what they were seeing. As Prince Leo's body began to arch forward, his feet began to rise off the ground. His body straightened and with outstretched hands he continued to ascend over the city until he could see the forces around the city. He could see the heads of men, women and children, even babies, on the end of spears and a tumultuous fire burst forth from within his chest. Then in his eyes, mouth and hands. Soon, there was a gigantic, ear popping explosion and the night sky lit up as if it were day. The entire sky it seemed was covered with fierce, raging fire. It seemed as if the now bright sky itself was burning in unquenchable flames and would be reduced to ash. The attacking armies, dismayed at what they were seeing with own eyes, were turning to leave but by then it was too late. The gleaming, glistering sky embroiled with flames fell to earth and washed them all away in its incinerating waves. The once imposing horde disappeared within a flash.

Slowly the fire began to dissipate into tiny flames and the bright night was soon dark again. The tiny flames flickered away leaving the vegetation unexpectedly unscathed. Not even a whiff of ash could be found anywhere and any sign that an army had ever ventured about the broken walls of Spes was erased, save the hoof prints of the horses. The night slowly became cool again and quiet.

Unknown to Fortis, he had wet his pants. His blood had frozen in his veins when Prince Leo had let out that roar. When he became conscious again, Prince Leo had been engulfed in flames high up above the city. Then there was an explosion and he went shamefully terrified. When the dark night sky ignited fire, his brain had refused to function and he was left abandoned by his senses. Now he was staring out the city walls and couldn't believe his eyes, his heart pounding faster than any natural beat.

Had he been dreaming, hallucinating? What was going on? What sort of madness was this? Had there ever been an army? Was this night real? Was he dreaming? Had he been dreaming? "Wake up!" he told himself. Where was that army that had been at their door? He could have sworn that there was an army out there and that there had been fire!

"You may put that sword away now Fortis. There would be no need for it."

Fortis turned around only to see Prince Leo calmly walking away. He didn't see any smoke around him. He didn't seem to be burnt up. He didn't look dead. He was actually here, alive and walking away.

Crying. He heard crying. Fortis headed over to a pile of broken beams and stone. His knees were shaking and he found it difficult to walk. His insides too were still trembling and felt like they were rolling down a steep hill. He lifted some of the beams to find Promptus curled up in a fetal position, shaking and crying profusely. He was covered in a cold sweat and his entire face was wet with tears and sweat. The poor child was bewildered out of his mind at what he had just saw and Fortis didn't blame him.

Then the stench. Horrified Fortis jerked away from Promptus. The boy had obviously lost control of his bowels too. Still, Fortis didn't blame the boy. Tonight was a night that they all would never forget.

He crouched behind a broken wall, looking on as Prince Leo walked away from Fortis. He, Procer, had been here in the city almost since the beginning as a spy, living among these people. He had seen and experienced first hand what these people went through and it broke his heart every single day. How he longed to be relieved of his post and to return to his home in Lux. But for the king, he would do anything and this, however, was where King Unus wanted and needed him at the present. He had been here secretly urging these people to the Testament of King Unus and the Standard of Light. But in very subtle ways, of course. There were hundreds like him all over the land of Nox, causing and helping the lost ones to see the glory of the light of the king, the One and Only King. One would have thought that it would be easy, taking into account the misery these people lived in . But Casus was efficient in his diabolical manipulation and ruthless cruelty. He kept these people blind and their spirits broken. So much so that to them it's a way of life, the only way of living that they know. Anything else is foreign, fearful.

Insurrectum Ex Lux Lucis

He hated Casus. He hated Casus for causing this pain and suffering. It wasn't and isn't necessary. Oh how he remembered that day when he received word that Sedes was being stormed. Both he and his troops were governing their assigned lands in the countries of Fertilis. He was about to march to Sedes immediately when his sister Voluntas reminded him that in his last meeting with King Unus, he had been ordered not to leave the countries of Fertilis until he was sent for by the king himself. Obviously, the king knew of what was about to happen. So, according to King Unus' wishes, he reluctantly remained. His entire soul however, yearned to be in Sedes, defending the city, defending the king. But he had to trust his lord's wisdom.

Soon word came that King Unus himself quenched the rebellion. It was discovered that it had been Casus who had been behind the whole idiotic plot and that he and his had been banished. How could Casus, loved, blessed and so mightily honored by the king, do such a thing? Was this what Casus had in mind when he had gone to visit him during the earlier seasons and complained that the lords, nobles and governors didn't have enough power? He remembered how he had asked Casus how much power he thought they all ought to have and why he thought it necessary. Casus mumbled something and appeared to be bothered.

There weren't any problems in the entire realm and on the contrary, there was peace and prosperity everywhere. Things always seemed to be progressing for the better rather than getting worse. The people were always fed, living happy, peaceful and productive lives. What else did Casus want?

He, Procer, had done his best to cheer up Casus, his guest, and make him enjoy his visit. But he nonetheless remained distant and departed before the set time that he had said he would leave. Had he, Procer, known what Casus was up to, he would have bashed his head in right then and there.

Well, no matter. The king was going to rectify everything. All the damage done to these people and the innocent children that were punished so unfairly, their justice would be meted out and by King Unus' mighty hand. But tonight, he was proud of his prince. The great prince, Lord of Sedes, Son of King Unus and the pride of Lux was here. Casus would taste the vile juices of his own craft and then be crushed by the forces of Lux. Prince Leo has started the rebellion that would spread all over Nox and redeem these people. Prince Leo will declare the Testament of the King and raise the Standard of Light. This was indeed a great day.

Chapter Six

The rebuilding of the city went smoothly and according to plan. Prince Leo, himself, laid out the blueprint for the new city. The one hundred sixty-one remaining inhabitants of the new City of Spes all chipped into the labor. The new city designs called for modern, spacious and luxurious buildings and mechanical innovations all specially thought up by Prince Leo in order to make life more comfortable and pleasant for the inhabitants. The first thing on the list for reconstruction was the city walls. Prince Leo knew that with the walls of the city came the people's pride in their city. With every man, woman and child contributing and so few people working so hard, side by side, day after day, the city soon became one big family. Parentless children found their way into the hearts of childless parents or single adults. Families were formed and marriages were preformed.

Frederick De Leon

The population of Spes began to grow. Not necessarily due to child birth but because many people were coming from surrounding cities, towns, villages, to see what was going on. There had been accounts of people seeing fire in the sky over Spes from other cities a great distance away and heard that armies from three powerful cities had been eradicated all in one night. Many of these inquisitive travelers were risking their lives to, first of all, find out if the stories were true, and second of all to see this strange, new leader in Spes and the great things being done there. Risking their lives because word had gone out all over the land it seemed, forbidding anyone to go anywhere near Spes. Those who were found on their way there in blatant disobedience to this decree were tortured, maimed or killed. However, nothing stopped the people. So often, those who dared to come see, being enthralled, stayed as well. They too could not peel themselves away from this man who did back breaking work with the people, designed beautiful houses for them to live in and at night, told them tales of a different and distant land of peace and happiness. Of how children were loved and cherished, fed and nourished. Women were adored and treated with respect and admiration. Where men were men, strong, courageous, honorable and fatherly. Of a king who made certain that his subjects had all things in order to insure life and sensible pleasure. Where there was a law that governed all and was fair to all and kept all things balanced and orderly. No wars and no tears of sorrows. Seasonal congregational feasts and celebrations before the magnificent gates of the glorious City of Sedes, the seat of King Unus himself.

The people wanted to hear more of this king who was coming to redeem them from their pathetic lives and miserable state. A king who brought with him a righteous creed and would unite all lands to himself. He would make Nox part of his lands and grant to them all the goodness he had given his other subjects. He would love them no less and insure that they were all filled with gladness all their days. These people swore oath to the Testament of the King and took the Standard of Light.

"My lord, should we not begin to build for you," Fortis came up to Prince Leo and asked one day as he was standing atop one of the buildings looking out over the city.

"There are spies amongst the people Fortis," Prince Leo replied.

"My lord?"

"You heard me. Casus has sent some of his people to corrupt Spes from within. What he can't have by force, he would take by subtlety."

"How do you know this my lord?"

"About the spies or Casus' workings?"

Fortis thought for a moment.

"The spies. You know them?"

Prince Leo turned and looked at Fortis. That was more than ample response.

"Discover them my lord. Bring them out and we shall destroy them or send them back. We have worked too hard to...."

"What you worked hard to build, work harder to maintain Fortis."

"But my lord, they will disrupt the people. They will seek to trouble your rule...."

"Your rule, Fortis."

"My lord?"

Now Prince Leo turned completely to face Fortis and looked him straight in the eyes.

"I am leaving Spes. I am going to other cities to meet other citizens of Nox. As I prepared you, I must also prepare them. I leave Spes in your hands."

Fortis was shocked. He was not ready for this. He was not able. It was not his place to be a ruler of a city and much more a city becoming great like Spes.

He was afraid.

"My lord, I can't. I am unable to...."

"Spes shall be left in your care Fortis. I leave on the morrow."

"My lord, the people...."

"Gather them this evening. I will speak to them."

"But my lord, I...I....."

"Fortis, I too have people all over Nox. Even in this very city, right now."

"You mean people from Lux?"

"Warriors. Mighty men."

"Here in Spes? But I know everyone," Fortis said struggling to believe his ears.

"They have been here in secret the entire time."

Fortis wasn't sure as to whether he was to be relived or even more frightened. What business was this? There were so many things going on that he didn't know about unless he was told or shown. So many things going on behind the scenes. But the truth was, as he was realizing, he didn't have a choice. One side would crush him and the other side would help him. It was that simple. Plus, if everything he had heard was true and if he believed the things he had seen since the arrival of Prince Leo, the side that would help him was stronger than the side that sought to crush him and his people.

His people. It felt strange that he, a nobody, should now think not only of his own welfare, but the welfare of these people who were now supposed to be his responsibility. And subverters were hiding in their midst?

"Don't be afraid Fortis. Everything will be alright. Trust."

"My lord, what of the little girl? What of Maeror?"

Prince Leo turned a few paces away from Fortis and stood with his back facing him. It was obvious that he was struggling with his emotions. Over the period of time that he had been in Spes, she had grown more and more attached to him. He had begun to see her too as his own child and now, he had to leave.

"My daughter is your daughter," he finally said. "I know she will be in good hands."

"I will do my best but it'll be difficult for her my lord."

"It's difficult for me too, Fortis. I would love to stay here with you all but there are others who must hear and follow. Spes shall be the gateway to Lux. To all willing, send them on their way to meet the king. Send them to the Seven Seas and the Seven Mountains. I will send leaders to lead the people in their way. Give them all you possibly can for the journey, both words and meat. But to them that are strong and seek to fight in the rebellion, send out to the cities of Nox. May the One King help us all."

Prince Leo walked away leaving Fortis wild with thought and fear.

Later that evening all the people were gathered at the same steps where Prince Leo had first healed them. They were now marble steps and were called the Steps of Leo. Many of the people gathered there had tears in their eyes but almost all of them had broken hearts. They knew why they were there; why they were called up in an assembly. Prince Leo was leaving them and going on to visit other cities of Nox. Though they understood why he had to leave them, they were far from glad about it. They had not yet heard enough words from this youthful yet wise and powerful man. They had neither seen him, nor touched him nor known him enough. But then again, how much of the charismatic Prince Leo would be enough for any person? Nevertheless, tonight was to be his last night with them.

Prince Leo came to the steps with Mearor on his shoulder. She was clinging to him and would not let go. He felt tears sting his eyes as he saw the people gathered and Mearor clung to his robe even tighter. It hadn't been long ago that this very same child had lost her parents. He had been the first one to pick her up and attempt to console her. And now, it seemed as if he too would be abandoning her to the cruelties of life in Nox.

Would she be strong? Would she softly cope? Would things be well with her?

Don't worry about the child, he could hear King Unus' voice say. *She will be well.*

Prince Leo climbed the steps slowly. As he ascended, he could hear the sobs behind him rise and increase in number. He not only heard but felt their heartache and tears flooded the rims of his own eyes and threatened to streak down his face.

Upon reaching the top, he turned and faced them. He now felt Mearor's little body shaking with sobs. He struggled with his own emotions as he looked into the eyes of the people. The eyes of the women who cooked and washed for him. The eyes of the men who cut down trees and built and designed buildings and had sweat with him. The eyes of the children who ran to him and loved him and had clung to him. The eyes of the few bent on destroying Spes and all that both he and the people had accomplished together.

Prince Leo whispered to Mearor and motioned to Fortis to come get her. She resisted at first but after some cajoling, allowed Fortis to take her. Prince Leo turned to the crowd and felt their energy. He felt every tear stream every cheek and felt every eye on him. He lifted his voice.

"We have been here, living here together, working together, loving and caring for each other. We have built what had been torn down and have carved diamonds out of coal. Where once this was a destitute city, it has now become a city of hope. Where so many perished, so many now and will continue to flourish. The Standard of Light has come to Nox and it all began here, in Spes. Wickedness shall be expelled from the entire land of Nox. Sorcery, conceit, arrogance and all types of villainy shall be eradicated. Peace, joy, tenderness and the crown jewels of virtue shall take their place. I, Prince Leo of Lux, will take all your sorrows from you when I introduce you to my kingdom. For now, however, I must see your fellows in the other cities. I must walk with them, laugh with them, talk with them, eat with them, mourn and cry with them as I have with you. I must be one with them as I have been with you, to know them and have them know me. To love them and give them chance to love me. Once upon a time, all lands were bathed in brilliant sunshine. The sunshine that comes from smiling faces and joyful hearts. For Nox, that was once upon a time. A darkness was produced from dark clouds which sought to blot out the sun. But light is stronger than darkness. Dark clouds are temporary but the rays of the sun always shine through. Like a knife, the rays of the sun have now cut through the dark clouds and have shown in Spes. The rebellion of the light has begun and soon all of Nox will be flooded, flooded with joyous hearts, sincere and heartfelt smiles, blissful thoughts, fulfilling wine. Nox shall be flooded with light."

Prince Leo looked out at them for one last time and descended the stairs. He would rest tonight and leave Spes early the next morning.

It was cold and dark. Mearor was still asleep by his side. His heart ached for this little girl. She had insisted that she spend the night with him last night. He was her only parent. The only one she truly trusted since her birth parents passed away. He wondered what kind of morning she would have when she woke up to find him gone? She had determined to stay up all night in order to see him go. But she had been overtaken by sleep a little before midnight. The poor child had worn herself out.

He got up soft and quietly so as not to wake her. He adorned his black robe, covered his head with the hood and stepped out into the dark, crisp morning. He was surprised to see people out all over the city holding torches. Fortis too was by his door awaiting him with a torch in his hand. He had with him a bag of provisions and a sheathed sword.

"My lord, I thought you would need these," Fortis said.

"Thank you Fortis. The sword though?" Leo said to him with a somewhat humorous grin.

"I didn't think you would need it but I thought still that you have it with you."

Fortis led the way to the stables. A procession of people followed with their torches in hand. They were soon at the stables where there were two horses prepared and harnessed.

"Why are there two horses," Prince Leo asked.

"Because I go with you," came a reply from the shadows.

"No. You may not Promptus," Prince Leo replied. "There is much danger. Stay here in Spes and be of aid to Fortis."

Promptus stepped out of the shadows and mounted one of the horses.

"My lord I go with you," he said again from atop the horse.

Fortis leaned forward to Prince Leo.

"My lord, I beg. Allow the boy. Even for me, I shall feel better."

Prince Leo looked into the boy's eyes. There was a man in there. A very, strong and determined man. A worthy man.

Prince Leo mounted his horse. He looked at the crowd, the torches and with one last nod to Fortis, he galloped out of Spes with Promptus in train.

THE CITY OF DESPERO

Chapter One

They rode until the sun was totally up and out behind them. The city to which they were headed was one of the cities that had sent troops to attack Spes. One of the cities that lost people in that attack. Prince Leo wondered....

A sharp pain pierced his arm. Prince Leo let out a shout and dropped down from his horse. It was an arrow.

"Promptus! Get down!"

Promptus jumped down off his horse and they were soon under a shower of arrows. Some of the arrows hit the horses and sent them galloping off in a frenzy. This left Prince Leo and Promptus exposed being that they were in open ground. Prince Leo took two more arrows in the chest and thigh. Promptus was hit twice in the stomach and began to bleed profusely. Prince

Leo reached out and grabbed Promptus' hand and immediately the bleeding stopped.

The arrow shower stopped momentarily and horses approached from almost every direction. It wasn't long before the two, lying on the ground in a pool of their own blood, were surrounded by soldiers. One of the soldiers ran up to Prince Leo and kicked him hard in the face. The last thing Prince Leo saw was blood before he lost consciousness.

Chains. Rattling chains.

"My lord? My lord?"

"Promptus?"

"Aye my lord. Are you alright?" Promtus asked.

"Yes I...I am fine."

Prince Leo squinted in the darkness to find the person with whom he spoke. It was useless and the air was foul. His hands and feet were bound in chains to the wall he stood or, more accurately, leaned against. His body was racked with pain, his head was throbbing and he was dizzy.

"What of you? Are you alright?" Prince Leo asked.

"No. My stomach hurts. Why didn't you do something?"

"I did do something. I stopped your bleeding," Prince Leo replied defensively.

"No. I mean like explosions and fires and those things."

"It wasn't time for that."

"But you got hurt and I got hurt. You have the power. I know you do. I've seen it."

"Is that what you expected? Is that why you wanted to come with me?"

Silence.

"No. I've sworn oath. I'll work for your king even if you had no power. I would still work the rebellion with you. It's all I have. But why have the power and not use it?"

Prince Leo's head was throbbing badly. How could he explain. He wasn't in the mood to explain. His entire body was enveloped in pain.

"There's a time for everything Promptus. Time to act, time not to act, time to react, time to endure. All in perfect time."

"I don't understand. So is this time to suffer?"

There was no reply. Prince Leo had passed out.

Prince Leo was awakened by the sting of cold water splashing against his aching body and into his fresh wounds. He clenched his fists and grit his teeth to keep from screaming out in pain. Then he felt at least five sticks pounding away at his wretched body. But what hurt the most were the cries of Promptus as he was also being beaten with clubs. After about a full thirty minutes, Prince Leo heard their tormentors leaving. Despite Promptus' whimpers and heavy breathing, they were immersed in silence.

"Promptus, how are you?" Prince Leo asked.

"I...I...don't know."

His voice was weak but laced with anger.

"How much sufferings must we take?"

"I don't know," Prince Leo replied.

"My lord, I think we are in Despero."

"I know we are."

Prince Leo could feel the blood rolling down his body.

"Promptus?"

"My lord," he was still breathing heavily and in great pain.

"Do you regret your decision to come with me?"

"No...no my lord."

"How much more of this do you think you can take?"

"I...I don't know my lord. I don't know. I'm afraid."

"But you would stay till the end of your strength?"

Promptus was getting annoyed. What did it matter? He was here wasn't he? He was suffering wasn't he? It wasn't like he had a choice. It wasn't like he could get up and leave whenever he wanted to. He was being beaten with clubs and chained and arrows had been shot at him. What choice did he have chained up in this dungeon? If he told the guards that he didn't want anymore, they still wouldn't let him go.

"Aye my lord. I would stay till the end of my strength."

"Let us leave this place Promptus."

Promptus was stunned when the chains that held both his hands and feet fell off him immediately. A hand grabbed him and, instantly, all pain he felt in his body was gone. He felt revived and strengthened. The hand, which he knew had to be Prince Leo's, pulled him and before he knew what was happening, they were walking through walls.

He was indeed frightened at first but then realized that there was nothing to fear. It didn't hurt when they passed through the stone walls. Actually, their feet didn't even make a sound on the floor they walked on.

It was as though they had turned into ghosts. The guards either didn't or couldn't see them and right when he was forgetting his fears and beginning to enjoy the experience, they were out in the middle of some alley under the moonless sky. Prince Leo had let go of his hand and was walking ahead of him. Promptus took a moment to gather himself and then ran to catch up. He wanted to ask about everything that had just happened. How did they do that? Would they do it again? But he didn't want to seem childish or look stupid. So he said nothing; he just followed.

The city was bustling with activity. To Promptus, the people were strange, very strange. Most of the people in the streets were either drunk or out of their minds in some way. They were falling over themselves and each other and appeared to be genuinely carefree. They were all stupid.

However, there were others who appeared terribly somber. They walked about teary eyed and seemed ever on the verge of releasing those tears. Their clothes and bodies seemed miserably unkept and they reeked of foul odor.

Question. How could two groups of people, so different, live together in one city. The drunkards and fools wore the best attire, embroidered in gold and silver threads, adorned precious stones and seemed, from their podgy stomachs, to enjoy the finest foods. Yet on the other hand, the somber, alert and apparently more intelligent were unkept, stank, dressed in rags.... What sort of madness was this?

Promptus was just about to ask Prince Leo when....

"We'll talk of it later," Prince Leo said to him.

Prince Leo walked through the crowd and went straight over to a hunched back, old hag who seemed unable to look up at him or anyone. Promptus heard him ask her.

"Do you await the 'coma'?"

"I am one who awaits the 'coma'," the hag replied and crossed the street while Prince Leo went down the alley nearest where the hag had been standing. Promptus followed him but could not see anything because it was so dark so he simply followed the sound of Prince Leo's footsteps. The sound of which suddenly stopped and a door opened, shedding some light into the dark alley and briefly blinding Promptus. Prince Leo grabbed him by the arm, hastily pulled him into the lighted room and closed the door behind them.

After squinting for a little while and trying to get his eyes to adjust to the light, Promptus scanned the room they were standing in. It was simple and bare. He was surprised to find that the only light in the room was from a single candle burning on a little table in the middle of a very small room. The room was furnished with only one small chair, a table and a bed in the corner.

"We will share the bed Promptus. I'll have it during the day and you by night."

"Oh no my lord. The floor is fine. I am used to sleeping on the floor. I shan't be offended at all."

"You have the bed tonight Promptus. You've had a long day."

Before Promptus could say another word, Prince Leo was out the door.

Hood over his head, Prince Leo walked the streets of Despero all night. He wanted to feel and know the soul of the people and their city. He wanted to understand their psyche. He saw people involved in sexual acts in the open public, with children out and about. There were drunk people, filthy people and they were all people of despair.

Prince Leo grabbed at a man on the verge of drunkenness. The man was finely dressed and wore gold and silver jewels.

"How is your future friend?" Prince Leo asked, disgusted by all he saw around him.

When the man opened his mouth, the stench of alcohol almost forced Prince Leo to buckle over.

"Future?! What future? What bloody future? You believe in a future? You're a bigger fool than you look. There is no future but destruction! That is the fate of all things living, friend! Death and destruction! Death and destruction to all! Heh, heh. Ha, ha, ha!"

The man began laughing and pouring the bottle of wine he had over his head, some of it splashing all over Prince Leo's face. Prince Leo, now filled with disgust, pushed him and he fell unconscious to the ground. Leo spat and began to walk away. Then he stopped, turned and looked at the heap of mess he left there lying in the street amidst the mass of people. A pathetic, pitiful idiot dressed like a king.

He went back, picked the man up, lifted him to his shoulders and carried him to the nearest alley. Prince Leo slapped him in the face a couple of times to rouse him up and leveled his face with his so that he could see directly into the man's eyes. The man stirred and Prince Leo shook him. His eyes began to open and as they did, Prince Leo's eyes began to glow. This startled the man who began to struggle but Prince Leo's strong arms held him in place. He began to squirm and shake and try to peel his eyes away but to no avail. The intensity of the light in Leo's eyes increased and the man became docile, staring into the brilliance. Soon, the man's own eyes began to glow.

Prince Leo blinked and the light in his eyes began to fade while the man's eyes continued to glow brighter. Prince Leo stood up and stared at the man, whose very countenance began to change.

"Your name is now Docere," Prince Leo said to him before disappearing into the night crowd.

The man remained there beholding light.

Chapter Two

Promptus awoke to see Prince Leo sitting at the table writing on a piece of parchment. There was a loaf of bread, a bowl of fruit, a pitcher of water and a wooden cup on the table.

"Get up and eat," Prince Leo said without looking up at him.

"Yes my lord."

Promptus was curious about a lot of things. For example, did Prince Leo know that they were going to be ambushed on the way to Despero? Did he know where exactly they were going to be ambushed and that they were going to be shot with arrows? Did he know beforehand that they were going to be arrested, imprisoned and severely beaten? Was that the way he devised to get into the city? And why did he choose for them to leave the prison at the time that they did? Why not before the beatings? Why after?

Besides, what kind of city was this anyway? Why were all its people bizarre? Some were extremely happy unto foolishness and others were solemn. Why? And who was the old hag in the street and what was the "coma" she and Prince Leo spoke about?

Prince Leo looked up at him and smiled. He began folding the parchment he had been writing on.

"Eat Promptus. I will need you to run an errand for me while I rest."

"Yes my lord," Promptus replied hurrying his way out of bed.

"Did you sleep well?"

"Aye."

"It's already started Promptus."

"My lord?" as he paused from biting into a piece of bread.

"The rebellion. Here. In this city. It has already begun. Is that not one of the many things on your mind?"

"Yes my lord. But how? Have we not only just got here? Only last night we came from prison."

"Promptus, think back and hard to before I arrived at your city. Was there not a dissatisfaction deep within your soul, long before you met me? A yearning for, if not better living, for a complete peace of being, a fulfilment that only eyes wide open could give? Did your heart and mind not know that your entire sight was dim and insufficient? Did you not desire to peel back the covering from over your eyes to see clearly the brilliance of the sun's light?"

Promptus thought. Strangely put, but it was true. He had often asked himself the question of whether it indeed was that he was simply born to sorrow all his life. He and his family worked the land like slaves for the people of Elatus. To the bone they worked their hands. Though his aunt and uncle loved each other, that love did not mask the pain of their hearts that life was not better, that life did not seem to hold much more. The very same people they had been killing themselves for eventually came and killed them. Those very people took from them until they took the very last thing they had, their lives.

Prince Leo touched his hand.

"It's alright Promptus. Let it go. Haven't we much work to do? We have rebellion to work among the people. Eat and get strength."

Prince Leo wanted him to give the parchment to a man named Docere. How was he expected to find one man out of an entire city of people? Moreover, they had only gotten about this city the night before. He didn't know his way around. Mightn't he lose his way and get lost somewhere in this strange, unfamiliar place?

Promptus was shocked to find the streets of the city just as lively and melancholy as the night before. He still didn't understand what was wrong with these people. Why did they act like this? So pathetic. Was this how his own people of Egenus looked before the attack and Prince Leo's arrival? Their state could not have been this bad. They were hard working people and had not had the time for happiness or dancing or any type of foolishness. They had to supply the people of Elatus with almost everything they needed. Their days had been filled with dread, sorrow, rigorous routine and exhausting work. Before he left, however, though they still remained a hard working and serious people, they found time to smile, to laugh, to sing and hear music. They could comprehend heartfelt joy. But these people on the other hand, he thought, they were just plain stupid.

Docere. Docere. Docere. How was he to find this man? The streets were just as crowded, if not more so, than the night before. Prince Leo saw how many people were out here. It would be impossible to find any one person. Promptus decided that he would search about for a little bit more and then return.

The boy looks down on the people of this city.

"Yes father, I know," Prince Leo replied. "That's how they all are here in this land of Nox. Everyone turns up the nose at everyone else in order to feel good about themselves. If they don't have somebody they think they're better than, then they have no self-esteem or sense of personal worth."

Well, that is wrong and I want it corrected. Need the boy be harshly reminded that in his beloved City of Egenus, their hard working people were too weak to defeat the few men from Elatus? That they were nothing but pitiful slaves? Need he be reminded that they all wallowed in sorrow and did absolutely nothing to free themselves? Where would they have been right now had you not been there that night after the attack? Where would he have been?

"Father, calm yourself. He will learn his lesson in time. He needs time to grow, to think. He has a lot yet to go through. Whether he knows it or not, he is merely seeing in these people a reflection of himself and his own people. Allow the light to shine father. Give it time to shine."

Promptus was sick of wandering about this weird city. The insanity of it all was beginning to get to him. He wasn't going to find Docere, or whoever that person was. Not today, not tomorrow nor any other day. The only thing now was trying to find his way back. He had tried to remember landmarks but it was hard to think or remember anything in all this noise, music and anarchy. He thought he remembered that....

Thud!

He was slammed to the ground. His head was spinning and he was in a daze. He looked around to see who it was that had hit him and realized that it was a solider. He was about to spring to his feet and bolt but noticed that the solider wasn't after him but was headed somewhere else. He was pushing people out of his way, trying to get somewhere. Then Promptus heard it.

"Let go of me! My name is Docere! There is light! There is hope! I have seen it! Let go of me!"

Promptus could not believe his ears. Cautiously, he headed towards the commotion, the same direction as the solider who had bumped into him.

"Let go of me! I must tell the people! I must tell everyone!"

Promptus could now see more soldiers trying to subdue the man.

"The stories are true! There is a king! His name is Unus! There is hope for the future!"

People were beginning to gather around, looking at Docere as though he was the most crazed person they had ever seen in their lives. There were only two soldiers upon the man but Promptus could see that there were more on their way. He felt the excitement rushing upon him. This was just one man but still, like Prince Leo had said, the rebellion had begun in this city. He knew that if he was going to have any chance of getting the parchment in his hand to this Docere, he would have to do something and fast. The two soldiers holding Docere were struggling to keep him restrained, but if the others got there, there would be no struggle. Then how was he going to get the parchment to him if he were locked up in prison?

Think Promptus! Think! He told himself. There had to be something he could do. He could still hear Docere screaming like a wild man.

"I know the truth! Why won't you let me tell the people?!"

Promptus saw a jug of wine in a drunkard's hand. Quickly, he grabbed the jug and pushed the drunk aside. Feigning to be drunk himself, he approached one of the soldiers from behind and smashed the jug into the back of his head. The solider toppled over and the other was tossed to the ground by Docere.

Their eyes met.

Promptus was shocked to find the man dressed as one of the fools in the street but recognized something different in the man's eyes. He knew that this man must have met Prince Leo.

"Stop him," they heard a solider shout out in the midst of the crowd.

"Here," Promptus said in almost a whisper to Docere. "Prince Leo of Lux is in the city and he wants me to give this to you!"

The man snatched it out of Promptus' hand and disappeared among the people. Promptus looked behind him, saw the soldiers nearly upon him and did the same.

Miles, one of the soldiers en route to apprehend Docere, thought he saw someone familiar. He thought he might be mistaken, but a young man who was brought into the city the morning before and locked up in the special cell. He and another man. He could not be certain but he thought to follow the boy. There was something very strange about him. He was definitely not from this city, not a native. And if that were true, where was he from and what was he doing here in Despero? The lad had a certain kind of awareness and purpose about him that could definitely be the cause of trouble.

After following and watching him for a while, Miles decided to take the boy to the prison in order to question him. However, he had to close the distance between them, first of all, to take hold of the boy. He was beginning to do just that when a drunk fell and vomited all over him. He was knocked to the ground, the drunk on top of him, and the jug of wine in the drunk's hand broke on the cobble stone street bathing him in wine. His rage nearly got the best of him as he beat the man unconscious in the middle of the street. He was disgusted and honestly couldn't stand the scent of himself, wine and vomit. He decided that this idiot would have to pay for the mess he made and also for making him lose the boy in the crowd. Shaking with anger, Miles dragged the unconscious man to the prison and locked him up in the common cell which already had close to fifty people in there.

"I'm going to get myself cleaned up and finish the job on you, you worthless pig," Miles said to the unconscious body and stomped off.

The unconscious man slowly sat up. Prince Leo lowered the hood off his head, looked at the fifty other people imprisoned with him in the cell and

Frederick De Leon
smiled to himself.

Docere knew he couldn't go home but he had to. He wanted his wife and daughter with him, especially when he read the parchment. He had to get them out of his house. He knew that was where the soldiers would be looking for him next and if they beat him there, they would stake it out and he might never be able to get close to his family again.

Struggling to get through the crowd as fast as he could, he thought about what he was doing, what he was getting himself involved in. This was crazy. The truth was, he didn't know what all this was about. He had no clue as to what he was getting he and his family wrapped up in. All he knew was that he felt it. Deep down inside, he felt it. In all honesty, though, before last night, he couldn't have cared about his family. He couldn't have concerned himself with the whereabouts of his wife and daughter, if they were safe or whether or not he might ever see them again. Half of the time he was in a drunken stupor and the other half of the time he was trying to sober up and tend to his business affairs. Make more and more money so that he could buy as much wine and enjoy himself before the final destruction. Why care or worry about anything when the destruction of everything and everyone was inevitable? Was that not the fate of the world?

No. Now he knew it wasn't. It wasn't the fate of everyone and everything. Some things last forever. In a peculiar and ponderous way, he knew that now. Love, for example, lasts forever. Truth lasts forever and there can be no truth without light. So therefore, light lasts forever.

Where was all this coming from? This clarity of thought, this lucid thinking? Where and how did he learn all this? Was it the result of last night? Or was it inside of him all along and only got awaken last night? Was it always there like glowing coals covered with ashes, only needing to be fanned into flames? If at all it had been in him all along, then it was within everyone. All people needed then, was a solid blast of wind to awaken the coals and rekindle the blaze.

Chapter Three

Docere was winded and out of breath when he got home. He called out to his wife and daughter but they did not respond. He searched every room but they were nowhere to be found. Well, the truth was that they were hardly ever home. But again, there was the possibility of the soldiers. Had they gotten to his house before he did and taken them away? He had to find them.

He rushed out of his house and again into the crowded streets. He didn't know where to look. Where did his wife love to spend her time? Where did his daughter meet with her friends? He didn't know. He was suddenly amazed to discover that he didn't know anything about his own family. The two people who were supposed to mean everything to him, his wife and his daughter. Whenever he had been sober in the head, he would spend all of his time at his business, trading, bargaining, lying and manipulating, trying to accumulate as much wealth and riches as he could before the worst happened. He had never cared about knowing people and where they loved to go to meet friends. How could that have been of any benefit to him? That was why soldiers were looking for him and he was in the open streets searching for his family without a clue as to where they might be. The family he called his but had never known.

Miles was fuming all along the way. He smelt horrible and was feeling ashamed. He would break whatever bones that drunk had left in his body when he got back to the prison, he kept on consoling himself. As many bones as it took to satisfy his rage. What did it matter anyway? What did anything matter?

He made two left turns on two different streets and was approaching his home when he saw...Caecus? That was the name they had been given at the prison when they were told to arrest him. They had been told that he was inciting a riot among the people and speaking insanities. When they got to the scene, the idiot was yelling that his name was Docere and that there was light or something of that sort. Light?! There was no end to the fools in this city.

Nevertheless, this was his opportunity to catch him and singlehandedly too. He crouched down low so that he wouldn't be easily visible. He began to approach Caecus, or Docere, or whatever his name was, carefully. He noticed that the man was searching the crowd. He appeared to be looking for someone. What a fool. He had just now narrowly escaped being arrested by soldiers, got away clean, and here he was out in the open, in the streets, midday, searching for someone else without any regard for his own safety? Miles instantly had an epiphany. He now knew how the world would end. Everyone would continue to get more and more stupid until the last man, a bumbling idiot, would do something extremely dumb and get himself killed in the process. Jump of a cliff perhaps or drown in a river or lake or something. And just like that, the end of everybody. How pathetic.

This was going to be nice, though. He was going to catch this guy, take out some of his anger on him, maybe knock out a couple of his teeth, and then take him to the prison. He got up close behind Docere and punched hard and deep into his lower back. Docere began to fall backwards into him but was forcefully pushed forward by Miles. Docere hit the stone street and cut open his chin on impact. The parchment fell from his hands as he rolled over and instinctively cupped his hands to his bleeding chin. He managed to see a solider over him and felt a solid kick crash into his ribs. He began to brace himself for worse when hands grabbed him from behind. Then he saw two hooded people jump the solider from behind and knock him to the ground. Before they ran off, one of them kicked the parchment into his face.

Promptus was about to turn into the alley when someone grabbed him by the arm. He turned to see who it was, half expecting a solider. Instead, it was a young man perhaps a little older than he was.

"Come join us. Leave the way of folly," the young man said with a very serious and dismal expression on his face. He, Promptus at once realized, was one of those melancholy people in the street who walked about always looking as if they were on the verge of tears. The young man had six others with him, four other boys and two girls. They were non-threatening however.

"Join you," Promptus asked. "Join you to do what?"

"Do what? You are not from this city are you?" the young man asked letting go of his arm.

Promptus felt a pang of fear stab at him. What was he supposed to say? Of course he wasn't from this city but at the same time, he couldn't exactly proclaim that he was from the City of Spes. That would be not much different than going up to one of the soldiers and asking to be arrested and thrown into prison.

"No. Uh. I am, uh, from no city. I, uh, am one of those that live out...."

"Ah, one of the poor uneducated," the young man offered.

"Yes. Yes, I'm one of those. The poor, uneducated."

"Then come with us and we will teach you the end of things. We will educate you."

Promptus wasn't sure what to do. They didn't seem as though they would cause a scene if he declined. Yet, he was standing right before the alley leading to his and Prince Leo's secret hide out. He couldn't call any attention, whatsoever, to that spot. He felt he had no choice.

"I would be glad if you would teach me. I am quite the fool. I have never learned before."

"It is our woeful duty to educate the illiterate and prepare them for the dire. You haven't been the first and you shan't be the last."

Trying his hardest to imagine how much he would regret this decision, Promptus went with them.

"Where has all your despair got you? Has it made you wise, strong, better or worse than your former selves? You all have nothing to look forward to and so, why not kill yourselves? Right here. Right now."

Prince Leo eyed them from the corner of the cell, pausing to let his words sink in. They shifted nervously. His words were like an arrow piercing their hearts. The reality of their situation. Something they had never really thought about.

"But we still want to live," an elderly man said weakly. "I still want to live."

"Why?" Prince Leo asked.

"I...I don't know," the old man replied, hanging down his head. "I just want to."

"Could it be because there is inside of you a spark of hope and its that spark, maybe, that makes the most miserable life still worth living? Perhaps you believe somewhere in the dark corners of your mind that there is a greater truth than the one you've known or think you've known? Maybe something keeps prodding you and telling you that you are important, that you are a part of a greater scheme of things, that you belong to a higher realm of living."

The silence as caustic. All eyes were riveted on him. This stranger in a dark corner of the crowded prison, sitting on the filthy floor.

"Yes."

They tore their eyes off the stranger and pinned them on the old man. Tears were rolling down his face as he stared into space.

"Its all true. I have hoped but never believed it could be true. All my life. So many, many sad years. So much pain and shame."

He turned his eyes on Prince Leo.

"Tell me it's true. Tell me what you say is true. Tell me, please! Tell me."

Prince Leo got up and slowly walked over to the old man. He knelt down before him and looked deep into his eyes. He reached out his hands to the old man's face and wiped the tears away.

"It's true," Prince Leo said.

The old man raised his head and looked at Leo. There was something in him that told him that it really was all true. There was an undeniable light that shone into his soul and awakened him. The old man could no longer contain himself. He embraced Prince Leo and began to sob uncontrollably.

Chapter Four

Miles was beside himself with anger. He grabbed the parchment away from his face and, as he rose from the ground, drew his sword. He was going to kill the fools who had jumped him. This was the second time today and this time, whoever they were, they weren't going to get away with it.

But "they" were nowhere to be found. He looked all around him and could find neither them nor the man he had been trying to apprehend. What was going on? Something strange was going on in the city and he had no idea what it was. It was almost like a conspiracy. An underground conspiracy. But conspiracy of or over what? What could anyone help or change? Trying to change anything or make anything better was a complete waste of time. Nothing in the world was ever going to really change. Before long, the whole, sick, demented, demoralizing game is going to end in a very fitting way.

Still, if there were people up to something in the city, he had to find out about it. He had to know what it was. What it was they were after and how they intended to get it. He....

His gaze shot straight to his hand. The parchment. It might be the answer to all his questions. Then cautiously, looking about him, he put it under his clothes, sheathed his sword, and, as casually as he could preform, headed home. Upon arrival, he locked the front door and closed shut the window shutters. Only when he was in his bedroom did he take the parchment out from under his clothes and hid it under the mattress of his bed.

He was excited and filled with anxiety. However, his discomfort in his filthy, disgusting clothes and pieces of armor was unbearable. Hastily, he went and washed himself and put on fresh, clean clothes. He shut the door to his bedroom and retrieved the precious parchment from its hiding place under his mattress.

He began to open it but then hesitated. What would he find? Would he discover a devious plot to overrun the entire city and slay all its inhabitants? Was one of the other cities beginning a plot to take them over? Perhaps even take over the entire land of Nox? Was this parchment a drawing of maps and sketches of military tactics? Perhaps the best thing to do would be to take the parchment to his superiors. How would they react? Or then again, perhaps they already knew of this plot? Perhaps they were intentionally keeping him and other officers in the dark. Or, then again, maybe they were part of it?

This is silly, he told himself. Instead of sitting around and burying himself in a pit of paranoia, he would simply open the thing and find out what kind of information it contained. He deserved it after all he had been through today. Besides, he could easily re-fold the parchment, take it to his superiors under the pretense that he had never seen what secrets it had written down inside. How would they know whether or not he had read it?

Miles' fingers worked themselves into an instant frenzy as he began to open the document. When he had it completely unfolded and open before him, he was shocked. There was nothing on it! There was absolutely not one solitary drop of ink on the entire surface. Was this some sort of perverted joke? Was someone playing some idiotic prank on him? What was going on? His eyes could not accept the void that lay before him and as he continued to intensely inspect the paper....

A sharp, sudden, intense bolt of light shot from deep within the parchment and into his eyes. Miles began to scream in pain but was so overcome that the connection between his nerves, brain and vocal organs was severed. He was unable to move or shout. He simply sat there while the razor sharp rays cut into his eyes in a steady stream. Tears were rolling down his face while the rest of his body remained transfixed. He couldn't think and the only thing he could feel were those blades of light slashing their way deep, deep into him.

Yet he wasn't afraid. It hurt terribly but he was strangely at peace. How?

In no time at all, Miles lay sprawled out on the floor of his bedroom unconscious.

"It is because the true nature of all things is darkness, that we must seek to become one with the ultimate darkness through melancholy. Sadness. We must strive to obtain a full comprehension of the destructive power of sorrow and its relatives. The reward of this strenuous discipline is equilibrium with the force of all things and thus, through this, comes perfect peace. Then, at the due time for the annihilation of all things, we would be its heralds and welcome it upon the world."

Promptus thought that his ears would spit blood if he heard anymore of this nonsense. Where in the world did these guys get this foolishness? He had been sitting calmly, trying to pass the time and sooner or later ask to be excused from this cursed gathering, but, he had been unfortunate and some of the poisonous venom had penetrated his hearing. What he knew passionately to be the truth, was boiling inside him, demanding to be unleashed. He was doing his best to hold it back and not bring any unwarranted attention to himself. But, this was one battle he found himself losing.

"Though it is not easy," the young man who appeared to be the leader, teacher of the group continued, "one must work to saturate one's entire being with sorrow...."

"Excuse me. Sorry. I am very sorry but please, excuse me," Promptus said interrupting him.

"Yes? The uneducated one wants to speak. I imagine you have had difficulty following the discourse. I apologize. No doubt you have a question."

Promptus wanted to strangle him but thought that for some reason,

Prince Leo would not approve. Instead, he just asked his question.

"I am wondering what value this... 'discipline' has in the face of death. I mean before the annihilation of all things."

"Well, one gracefully submits knowing that one has practiced to unite with the iron fist of despair. So instead of being a victim of the hand, you become part of the hand, an everlasting office."

Promptus wanted to scream, but he didn't.

"May I ask your name?"

"My name is Praeco," the leader responded.

"Praeco, what if what you say is actually the exact opposite? What if, instead of darkness being the true nature of all things, what if it were light? What I mean to say is that, what if light really is the true and basic nature of all things."

All eyes fastened on Promptus.

"What," he continued, "if all things were crafted in magnificent light and set to motion? What if beautiful light more glorious than the sun, lay deep within the basins of all things but its radiance is clouded by thick dark clouds? We all know that dark clouds don't last forever and so what if that ever-present brightness lay in dormant state to be awakened, rekindled? What if it is the mighty sun that will, in soon time, pierce all darkness, sorrow, melancholy and despair and dominate all once again in everyplace?"

Praeco stood there staring at Promptus for a spell, his mind desperately trying to perceive what he had just heard. He had never heard anything like it ever before in his life, so simple yet so revolutionary. He tried to grasp the ramifications of such an ideology, if at all possible. Could it be that true, sincere, pure joy, incorruptible light and infinite gaiety instead of dismal paths, insatiable, infinite sorrow and melancholy would be the basic constituent of the almighty powers?

His eyes blinked. He was staring at someone. Who was it? He wasn't sure. He was having a hard time recognizing the face. Oh! Yes. It was the uneducated, the one from without the cities. He was staring back. Why? Everyone was looking at him. Why? Oh, it was because he was standing before them. He had been speaking to them, teaching them. But, right now, he didn't feel like teaching anyone. He didn't feel as though he knew anything. He wanted to be alone. He wanted to think. He felt like learning.

Praeco turned out of the meeting and walked away.

"I don't believe it? I don't believe any of it," said one of the men in the prison cell. "It's all rubbish! Wishful thinking."

"Perhaps it seems to be wishful thinking because you wish it were true," Prince Leo said to the man.

He mumbled something unintelligible. Then he burst out.

"Stop! Stop it! You're playing mind games. Just stop right now!"

Prince Leo could see that the man was trembling. He was confused and hurt. He was in pain.

"Dolor," Prince Leo called to the man with his hand out to him.

"Wait. How did you know my name? No one here said it. No one here knows it. How did you know my name?"

"The same way I know the truth," Prince Leo replied.

"Are you from the City of Magus? Do you practice sorcery," the man demanded.

"No I am not from Magus. I am from Lux."

This startled many of the people in the cell, those who had heard the tales, the myths.

"The legendary land of Lux," the man asked with a smirk on his face. "That's just a fairy tale for scared old women who don't want to accept the truth about the world and how its going to end. I'm not afraid. I'll meet the final darkness the way a true man ought to. I don't need your stupid stories."

"Suit yourself," Prince Leo said and raised his right hand to the huge iron bars and chains behind which they were all locked. Slowly, they began to disintegrate into smoke. The people in the cell gasped and ran to the opposite wall, away from the iron bars in shock and amazement. Within no time, the iron gate, bars and chains and smoke all disappeared into thin air. Prince Leo turned to the people.

"There is nothing keeping you here against your will."

One by one, they began to file out of the prison until the only ones left were the old man, Dolor and Prince Leo. The old man said to Leo.

"I have nowhere to go."

"But you have a lot to do," Prince Leo replied. "You have a new life to live."

The old man tried to smile and hurried out the prison.

Prince Leo turned to Dolor.

"Are you staying?"

"Aye. I don't need you and your... your...whatever it is that you do. The others may need your help but I do not. You just go. Go help the weak. They will most likely take you with your fantasies."

Without saying anything else, Prince Leo turned and walked out of the prison. As soon as he left, smoke reappeared out of nowhere and began to fill the prison cell. Dolor could see the outline of the iron bars and chains begin to form again. He quickly ran out of the prison before the iron bars and chains could materialize.

Chapter Five

Where was he? What was he doing here in this alley? And that pain. Agrh!

It was his chin. That solider hit him and he fell on his chin. Split it open. Good thing it stopped bleeding. He could have probably bled to death.

The parchment! Where was it? He couldn't have lost it. Then again, he most likely did when that solider attacked him. The kid who gave it to him said that a Prince Leo was in the city and wanted him to have it. Who was this Prince Leo? Could he have been the same man who had drastically transformed his life the night before? He had remembered hearing stories long ago about the Kingdom of Lux whose prince was named Leo. Could this be the very same one?

He couldn't believe he'd lost the parchment and he wondered what could have been in it. What profound information had it held and how could he have been so careless with it? And, he had almost forgotten. Who were those people who had come to his rescue? Where did they come from and why did they help him?

For now, he had too many questions and too few answers. What he did know for certain was that it was going to take more than near arrests and a split chin to shut him up.

"It should."

What? Docere struggled to turn again to see who it was.

"Who's there," he asked but already knew. How could he ever forget that voice.

Prince Leo stepped out of the shadows of the alley and into the light where Docere could see him. Docere didn't know what to do. He struggled to get up and in the process, upset his blood clotted chin. Blood began to pour. Prince Leo stretched out his hand and touched his chin. There was no more blood. Docere touched his own chin. It was as good as new, unshaven though.

"I...I lost the parchment," Docere told Prince Leo, feeling guilty.

"Don't worry. It's doing its work."

Docere was nervous. He felt like he was going to wet himself. This man, this very man standing before him must be Prince Leo. But why was he here? Why was he here in Despero?"

"The..." Docere swallowed. "The stories about Egenus, that was you?"

"Yes. And the story of Despero and five other cities will also be me. However, Egenus is no longer the name of that city. It is now called Spes as this city shall be called Visus."

"Visus," Docere echoed softly.

"Yes, Visus and you will be its ruler."

"Ruler? Ruler! No, no. I can't...."

Prince Leo raised his eyebrow at Docere. Silence issued and lingered for a while.

"Look at your city. Look at its people and the despair in their eyes. Think of the children who grow up knowing nothing but that despair just as you grew up captive to its altar. Think of your own child. Then think of the child your child shall have. Do you still tell me no Docere?"

Docere lowered his eyes to the ground before him. He was afraid, very afraid of what lay before him. Him, one of the city's thousands of idiots and drunks.

"You are not the same Docere," Prince Leo interjected.

"But that's all I've known my entire life. How could I rule anywhere? I haven't a clue."

Prince Leo began to turn and walk away.

"You have both the Standard and Testament in your heart. You needn't much more."

In his dark robe, Prince Leo seemed to disappear into the night.

Okay now he had to get out of here. He had opened his big mouth and said some things he probably shouldn't have said. He wondered if Prince Leo would be mad at him?"

He slowly got up and headed for the path back to the city's streets.

"Hold it."

Without turning around to see who had spoken to him, he replied.

"I'm sorry. I must leave now."

Promptus quickened his pace. He couldn't get anymore caught up then he already was. What if he caused problems for the rebellion? What if he had spoken out too boldly and too soon? Perhaps he shouldn't have gone to that meeting. But he couldn't let people discover their hiding place. For sure, the soldiers were looking for both he and the prince.

He heard footsteps behind him. It must be someone from the meeting. He wondered who it was but didn't want to risk looking back.

"Hold on. What's your name?"

From the sound of the voice, he could tell it was a girl. Why did she want his name? To report him? Maybe she was the daughter of one of the soldiers. There was no use in running now anyway. She was right behind him. Maybe if he simply gave her a name, she would go away and stop following him. Go away and report him. More beatings and suffering in that dreadful prison. He shuddered at the thought.

Promptus stopped and turned around. It was a pretty girl about his age. She was winded and seemed harmlessly curious. He hoped.

"I...I just...."

She was trying to catch her breath.

"I just wanted to talk to you. I've...I've never heard anyone talk like you did."

Promptus looked around. They were out in the open and he didn't like that. There were some trees to the right of them.

"Come," he said to her, grabbing her hand and leading her off to the cover of the trees.

Dolor lead an armed bunch throughout the city in search of Prince Leo. He'd be damned if he allowed that sorcerer to sneak into the city and corrupt it with his lies and sorcery. That fellow must be a rogue medicus from the City of Magus coming here to o'ertake Despero. He, personally despised the medicum and their strange mystic ways. Bizarre things they did. That was a sentiment that a lot of other people shared all over Nox. Everyone was afraid of those medicum. Well, he and his friends will find the fellow and kill him in the streets.

"There is a rogue sorcerer in Despero! He is trying to o'ertake the city? Out with him! We will have his head!" Dolor shouted amidst the crowd in the streets, drawing attention to himself and increasing the throng in his wake.

"We demand his head," someone else shouted.

"Out with him," said another.

"Take his life now and not wait the horrid future."

"He shall be our joy afore our own dark time," Dolor continued, further inciting them.

He wondered where he could be? Where was the sorcerer? Was he around? Was he hiding or perhaps even watching them?

A garrison of soldiers began to approach Dolor and his mob. He stopped and everyone else stopped with him. He was suddenly scared and didn't know what to do. He hadn't thought this far. Somehow, he had assumed this whole thing would have been over by now. They would have found the sorcerer, killed him and dispersed before soldiers could ever arrive and inquire as to what had happened. Obviously, it hadn't worked out that way. A whole mess of soldiers were now approaching him and he was stuck. Were they coming to re-arrest him for beating that old wench or for this mob he had summoned? He tried to judge from their faces, read their eyes. It wasn't working.

His palms were wet and his armpits drenched. His heart began to race and his knees were shaking. He knew that he was now at the point of no return and that there was no turning back. And thinking of the mob at his back, thoughts began to rise in his head. Interesting, intriguing thoughts. Thoughts that whispered in his ears, "Perhaps you can defeat these soldiers. And if you can defeat these soldiers, why not others. With a little luck...you might even be able to take the city. With this mob, right here, right now, this may very well be your chance and it will never come again. You might after all do something with your life. Become great. "

The adrenaline began to thrash its way throughout his body. It began to flood his brain, his eyes, his nose, mouth and hands. He became a sitting bag of explosive powder ready to blow. He waited for them as they approached.

The commanding officer began to grin at him. They called this one Fletus and almost everyone in the city knew him. He was originally from Scelus and was as wicked as they come. He had afflicted many tortures in the prisons that were beyond comprehension. It was said that he often sat around dreaming and imagining new atrocities in his head. Dolor felt a tingle in his back. The place where a huge chunk of flesh was missing. Missing because this man had felt it was necessary for it to be missing.

Praeco bit into his apple as he leaned against a building, watching the scene unfold. Though a safe distance away, he could see the eyes of both men. Though young, he was smart, intelligent. He could tell that something was about to happen, something big. Here. Right here. Right now.

He focused his gaze on the man leading the mob. The mob. The mob represents the people and more often than not, the future lies in the hands of the people. Rulers come and go, but the people. Ah, there's always the people.

Praeco shifted. His right arm was going numb as he had been leaning heavily on it propped against the wall. He wanted to be ready. He was already planning in his mind. He would watch this issue out and then, at the right moment, join the fray if he thought he had a chance to swing things. He would get involved at a crucial time and establish his place. He would prove himself to the leader there and with his oratory powers, snatch a prominent post in this...mob. Or with the soldiers maybe. Didn't matter. He would put himself close to power.

Again, he scrutinized the leader of the bunch. He was nothing more than a common brigand. He, Praeco, was young, he would admit that. But that only meant he had time. More time to grow. Make more of a name for himself. Perhaps even, one day, seize total control of Despero. Make it into a bigger and better city than the pathetic town of fools it now is. And as for that uneducated country filth who made a fool of him at his own meeting, he shall never forgive nor forget the insult. He would take pleasure in joining this motley band, maybe, or even the soldiers, and hunting down the members of this strange new sect. This city had its own traditions, its own beliefs that date back to the earliest time. They couldn't allow strangers to come in and inject whatever ideology they chose. A sorcerer from the City of Magus is what the leader of the mob had said. Most likely that uneducated country boy is in league with him. If they did plan on taking over the city, they would have needed to come up with some new, radical idea. Very much like the one he had heard earlier today.

"Come on Dolor. Let's go. Come calmly and I shall try not to have too much fun with you and your friends," Fletus threatened, trying his hardest not to laugh.

"I am going to kill you Fletus," Dolor responded, choking with anger.

He hated this man. He really hated this man. He wished he had something in his hand to hit him with. Perhaps a board or an iron rod. Wham! Right across the head.

"Come on! Give it up. You know its hopeless."

Dolor could feel fear now creeping into the mob behind him. He was waiting too long and they were interpreting his hesitation as fear. Fear in him would be multiplied in them. So, he lunged forward and swung. He missed his target but, his action was all the mob needed.

Praeco smiled. He liked what he saw. He liked it a lot. He began to laugh out loud. He threw away the apple core and looked around, searching the area for a weapon or a stick, something. He couldn't find anything. There was a blind man about ten feet away from him. He raced over to the man, who was trying to get away from the noisy commotion in the streets. Praeco tried to snatch away his cane. The poor man, fearful and not knowing what was going on or who was wrestling with him or for what reason, resisted. In the midst of this, Praeco was shoved from behind by one of those involved in the street tussle and fell backwards, bumping his head against the wall. He winced in pain. Struggling to get up, he saw a figure, dressed in a dark robe, atop the building across the street. Who was that? He had never seen the likes of him before. Who was he and what was he doing atop the building?

It seemed...if he was not mistaken, the person, it seemed a man, was looking directly at him. Staring was more like it. Staring at him. Why? Of all the more interesting things going on in the street, why was he staring at him?

Praeco got up, slowly. He didn't take his eyes off the man and the man didn't take his eyes off of him. He was getting nervous. Who was that man and why was he staring at him?

He turned his face away and stared at the ground before him. A woman fell into him and almost toppled him over. He made a conscious effort not to look back up at the man atop the building. The fight continued in the street before him but his mind was elsewhere. Unable to bear it any longer, he raised his head but saw only the clear sky above the building.

Someone else fell into him, heavily. They both fell to the ground. Praeco saw a solider with his sword raised and ready to strike. Out of sheer instinct, he reached out for something, grabbed a hold of it and swung. The cast iron pot flew out of his hands and smashed into the face of the solider who immediately fell backward and didn't get up. With sincere gratitude, the man who had fallen onto him, smiled at Praeco through a bloody face. Praeco recognized him as the leader of the mob.

Chapter Six

"How can you be sure of what you're saying? How do you know that its not all wishful thinking?"

Promptus noticed how cute she looked. Those large sincere, inquisitive eyes of hers, searching for answers, for reason. He looked at her lips that seemed both a subtle, yet, vibrant pink, moist and inviting.

"How can you be certain that what I tell you is wrong?" he asked Mitis in return.

She looked away.

"I don't know. No one knows for sure."

It was getting dark, getting late. A cool soft wind was blowing gently. Somehow there seemed to be a certain sweetness in the air. There was a calm.

"Close your eyes," Promptus said taking her hand in his.

"What?"

"Close your eyes."

Mitis closed her eyes, her hands in Promptus' hands.

"Do you feel that?"

"Feel what?"

"Just listen. Awaken every sensory organ in every part of your body."

Silence.

"Pay attention Mitis. Pay close attention to the entire world around you."

She sat there for a while, feeling the gentle breeze around her. She thought all this was bizarre but figured it was worth a shot. It was a nice evening. There seemed to be a subtle aroma, fragrance in the layers of the wind. She could hear the soothing rustle of the leaves and branches of the tree above them. Almost like it had come alive. Almost like it was speaking.... No, perhaps humming or singing or something of that nature. It didn't feel melancholy. It was just a sound. More joyful than dreary though. Music that just seemed to ascend sublimely into the evening sky. Higher and higher. She wanted to be a part of it. The music. The song. The sound.

She reached out and touched it. The sound of everything. The song of everything. In jubilation. In praise the song was sung. In harmony. In order. And enveloped in light. Splendid, cool, sweet, sparkling light. A motion. Movement. Flowing dance. In order. In unison, together.

She opened her eyes and smiled at Promptus.

Insurrectum Ex Lux Lucis

Docere didn't know what he had gotten himself into. An armed rebellion had arisen in the city and chaos reined everywhere. A man named Dolor and those with him routed half the troops in the city and was on the verge of gaining complete control. Some of the soldiers and people were fighting to maintain the former order but the idea of a king was too enticing. Perhaps exciting was more like it. Everyone looked forward to a dismal future. Having a king seemed one spark of light in their dark world. They said that this Dolor was a common criminal and that he had been arrested numerous times before. Now he was on the verge of becoming king of Despero. King of a city where everyone was full of despair, frustration, depression. What would King Dolor do?

He, Docere, walked through the streets freely. He was in the part of the city that was under Dolor's control. There were no soldiers to threaten or chase him down. Also, the people over here wouldn't recognize nor even think about him. No one cared about a crazy man in the streets earlier screaming about hope. And if they did, they would probably think this revolution was the hope he was talking about.

He wondered about his wife and daughter. Were they safe in the midst of all this madness? What did they think of it all? Which side were they on? What were they doing? Were they worried, concerned or even thinking about him?

He thought about the change in his life, the clarity of vision, the light that entered his head, the thought of the hope and optimism he had felt for the future. How things would look better and bright. But right now, he felt that things couldn't be worse. His life had been radically changed by a stranger who claimed to be the Prince Leo of Lux. He had filled his head with thoughts of being king of the city while it was a common criminal who seemed to be making a no nonsense trip to a throne of sorts. The city was in chaos and, worse of all, he had no idea where his family was.

What if all this was just some bad dream? What if he had had some pretty crazy stuff to drink last night? What if there was simply something messing with his head and he needed only to arouse himself from sleep and everything would be back to normal. Normal. What was that anyway? The life he had been living? Not caring about anyone, drinking himself into a stupor every night because he saw nothing luminescent on the horizon of his life? Normal?

No. This...this is real. What he was feeling right now. What he was knowing right now. This is as real as it gets. As best as it gets. Even if it hurts like nothing had ever hurt before, it was his hurt and pain that assured him that he was alive, alive for the very first time.

He stopped in the middle of the street, people brushing past him. He took a deep breath. Alive. For the first time. A tear came to his eye.

Someone bumped into him. It was then that he noticed that almost everyone was headed in the same direction. He stopped a lady hurrying beside him.

"Excuse me, where is everyone headed?"

She gave him a weird, quizzical look as if he were mad for asking.

"Acerbus Square. Where else? A leader of the revolution speaks."

She didn't hesitate to end the conversation and hurried ahead. A leader of the revolution was speaking in the square? This should be interesting,

Docere thought to himself. He could still hear the noise from the fighting in a distant part of the city if he listened closely. However, already they were consolidating their base. Smart move. Very smart move. And they said that the leader of this movement was a common brigand? Or, it could be that he had someone with him who possessed talent, brains. Someone who didn't want to be on the front lines fighting, risking his life, but wanted to be seen and heard by the people. He ought to hear this "leader" for himself.

He walked with the throng to the square. Walking and blending in with its fast paced stride. There was a high level of excitement and anticipation in the air. Two things that were very rare in Despero. These people had known nothing but despair since the days of their birth. Dismay at the dismal, black future. But here they were, listening to the already resounding voice of an impressionable, eloquent young man.

"It is time that we rise to meet our fate, instead of cower from it. It is time that we embrace it, feed off it, allow it to strengthen and empower us. It is time that we become one with our destiny.

"What do we know of the things to come? Nothing really. All we have is the past by which we can gauge the future. We have experience. What has changed between the past and the future. Nothing. Nothing really. And so we must, using our intelligence, dare to assume the fact that nothing is going to happen between the present and the future. So what, again I ask, does the future hold for us, our wives, children, mothers and fathers?"

Praeco, the speaker, paused for effect.

"The same thing we've known since we've entered this world! Sorrow! Despair! Melancholy! And finally, in the final end, the ultimate destruction that shall envelop us all. Digest us all."

There were moans and gasps of fear from the crowd. Docere saw children cling to their parents in terror, wives holding on to their husbands for a vain sense of comfort. And for the first time in his life, he wanted to do something to help these people, something to liberate them for the dark cloud that perpetually hovered over their lives. Perhaps pierce that cloud with a ray of light.

"He's good isn't he?"

Prince Leo didn't respond.

"My lord? Prince Leo? I said he's good, is he not? I am eager to know what you think of the young man," Casus' voice laced the air.

Only Prince Leo, of course, could hear him. Standing there in the square, amongst the crowd, twenty paces behind Docere, Prince Leo too was listening to the speaker.

"My lord?"

I hear you Casus, Leo replied without moving his lips.

"Then would my lord grace his servant with a response?"

Are you my servant Casus?

"I am your majesty's humble servant."

Then shut up.

Silence issued.

"You ought to go back to Lux, Prince Leo of Lux! You ought to turn around and go back! Perhaps you haven't noticed, but there is nothing you can do here. I've already beaten you to it. I will give them the hope you dragged yourself down here to give them. I will give them the inspiration to keep on living and living under MY rule. I will give them every possible thing you could ever give and they are going to take it on my terms. I rule here Leo. I am king. I am god. I am....."

Casus, I thought I told you to be quiet.

Prince Leo walked amidst the crowd and out of the square. Everything was going as planned.

"But today," the speaker continued, "men have been born. Leaders have seen a revelation of their true destiny. Our true destiny. Our rightful place in the final leveling off of things. We are here to lead you to the path of the only glory. We are here to show you a better way. The only way.

"The hope we have and must have is that of adaptation. When wise men are confronted with the inevitable, they realize that their only salvation from it is that very thing that is inevitable. Therefore, let us embrace the end. Let us welcome the final day with open arms. Let us bring it into our homes, into our lives, into our hearts. Let us become one with its infinite power of inevitability and let it give us life. It shall be the food we eat and the wine we drink. It shall become part of us and even embed itself in our very souls. And after that, when shall we ever be destroyed? By whom or by what? When we have become one with our own destruction and it is one with us, shall we not all be immortal? Shall we not be gods when we are no longer mastered by despair but we *become* despair? Shall we not be everlasting when we feel no sorrow but *become* sorrow? This is your greatness, o great and mighty City of Despero! Ye city of gods! Follow it! Yield to it and to your destiny and let us lead you to the end and beyond to forever!"

A thunderous noise arose from the crowd and filled the square. It was so mighty that it felt as though a giant had sat up and filled the entire square with his massive body. There was a ferocious electricity in the air and it charged everyone. It was as though all the people were one, one purpose, one destiny, one resolve. Yes. Indeed he was happy. Indeed he was satisfied, fulfilled. This was what he was meant to do. But as Praeco stepped down the makeshift podium, he knew it wasn't all him up there. Something had come over him.

Promptus heard the roar in the city and wondered what was going on. He and Mitis had parted ways a little while back and now, as he approached the city, he was concerned for her safety. But then again, if anyone was in danger, it was him. She had grown up in this city. She knew her way around the city. He on the other hand, didn't. He was a stranger here and an obvious one too.

As he entered the crowded streets, he was grateful that it was dark. He wouldn't be easily recognized by the soldiers. Also, he didn't want to be picked off by anyone of the other young people in that stupid meeting. Anyone of them could have him arrested for opening his big mouth and saying some of the things he had said. He decided to go home or to whatever it was that they had. Room? Hideout? But whatever it was, it was hard to imagine that he, Promptus, was actually sharing space with Prince Leo. Prince Leo of Lux! The actual son of King Unus. It was simply unbelievable. No one would have believed him had he told them a while back that at this very time, he would be in the personal company of someone like Prince Leo. This was greatness. He, Promptus, was a legend. He was already a legend. The name of Promptus would be highlighted in scrolls and books and volumes. He was a great man.

And Mitis. Ah! What would she think if he told her how close he was to the prince, rightful heir to all lands? How would she look at him then? Perhaps with more affection? Definitely with more affection. Admiration even? Now that would be splendid.

Did you hear Leo?! Did you hear?

It was Unus, his father. He had been listening to Promptus and was obviously upset.

"I heard father. And you're right. I see no reason why it shan't be so. Besides, now is the perfect time for them."

Well, regardless of that cause their union is part of the plan. But he is going to destroy himself and others if he continues this way. He is meant to be great but he could end up becoming a great harm.

"Sure," Prince Leo replied. "We'll just give him time to think. He'll be fine. Just a good bit of time in solitude to really think and reflect on himself. That ought to be good for him."

Promptus opened the door and had his eyes blinded by the light. He cringed and covered his eyes and almost closed the door without stepping in. He wondered how was it that a solitary candle could produce such powerful and forceful light.

"My lord?"

The glare began to dissipate and he began to uncover his eyes. Prince Leo was sitting at the table behind the lighted candle. Promptus could not see his face.

"I...uh...."

What was it again he had gone out to do? He'd forgotten how he began the day. He was at the meeting and that crazy fellow was teaching....

"The parchment Promptus."

Huh? Parchment? What parchme....

"Oh yes. The parchment. I found the man. I have forgotten his name but I found him. He was preaching in the streets. It was dangerous my lord cause the soldiers were upon him. I helped him escape after I gave the parchment to...."

"I know what happened Promptus."

"You do?"

"Yes Promptus, I do."

How did he know? How could he know? He wasn't there. Well perhaps he was able to....

"I'm leaving Despero Promptus. My work here is done. Everything is in place. Tonight, I leave for the City of Dubito."

"Wha...my...."

Leaving?! Now? Tonight? Why? No. They just got here. Just...when, uh, yesterday or was it the day before. Mitis. He had just met her. Leave her? Now? He wouldn't be able to tell her. She....

"My lord, did we not just get here? Surely, there is more to do."

"Of course there is. Not by me however."

He was crushed. He was devastated.

"Well, I suppose we must prepare."

"You need not."

Need not?

"My lord?"

"I go alone Promptus. It is as you said. There is yet much to be done here. Despero shall be changed, transformed into Visus. From a city of despairing souls to a place of vision where the people see through despair into the truth and the abundant flow of purity. The Standard of Light Promptus. The Testament of the King. Do you remember these?"

Like a knife. Those words cut like a knife. The question hit like a hot blade through a cake of snow. The Standard. The Testament. They seemed foreign to his mind. Like something long forgotten and yet they were the very reasons why he was here.

He suddenly felt naked. Bare. He...was ashamed. When and where had he gone off course? At what exact moment had he lost focus?

"Promptus," he heard Prince Leo's voice call his name.

He looked up. He had not even realized that he had lowered his head.

"It's alright. It happens. We move on. It is as you said. There is much to do. Much too much to wallow, don't you agree?"

Prince Leo smiled. It was contagious. Promptus smiled too and suddenly felt warm inside. It was okay. He would move past this and beware to never make the same errors. To never forget his focus or to ever put himself before the everlasting truths.

Praeco had needed some time away and so he took it. He was accustomed to being alone and having time with his thoughts. What he did out there today wasn't just impromptu. His speech was a result of hours in solitary juggling of ideas and rationalizations and explanations around in his head. Thinking was his specialty. It was what he did. But it wasn't an end in itself. There was a point to it all. A purpose. He had always had that nagging pain of a drive to find "the answer". The perfect solution to all equations. Simply put, the answer.

He smiled to himself.

Some of their soldiers passed and nodded respectfully to him as he strolled the city's walls; on their side of the city of course. Their soldiers. It sill sounded funny to him. Yesterday, he was just one of the many young men in the streets, peddling ideas to his peers. Today, he was one of the leaders of the revolution. After saving Dolor's life and that initial battle subsided, Dolor told him to stay close. Fight by his side. But Praeco knew better. Although he had saved his life, he knew that he was no fighter. Suppose he went into battle and something happened to him or he got killed? No. That was too much to risk. He had a greater purpose in life and he was determined to seek it out. He told Dolor that he would be of service best by rallying the people to their cause and consolidating support. He told Dolor that this was a crucial time and that if they played everything right, they ought to have control of the city in no time. He further explained to him how the people were confused and uncertain about what was going on around them. They needed a cause and a cause they could believe in. They needed something bigger than themselves and that he, Praeco, could supply just the thing. Dolor had stared at him perplexed but then smiled and patted him on the back. He knew he was out of his league with such things and that he ought to entrust that aspect to his young friend. So he did.

So while Dolor the Dullard went off to fight with the soldiers in the streets and risk his life, Praeco arranged to speak to the people and give them an explanation for what was happening in the city. It was amazing, though, to see how readily the people followed Dolor. It was as if they had always known him and trusted that he would liberate them. But there was a problem. A problem that Praeco instantly had the foresight to detect the moment he saw the initial stand off in the street. Yes, Dolor could fight the soldiers and perhaps even defeat them. But that was all he could ever do, fight. When the fighting was over, what then? That was where he came in. Dolor had the arm but not the head. Tonight, he, Praeco, proved that he had the head. It was he who truly liberated the people. It was he who breathed new meaning into their lives and gave them something to live for, someone to look up to. It was he who....

Who were those two and what were they doing on the city's walls? They didn't look like any of their soldiers and....

That was the man! The man on top of the building earlier today! The one who was staring at him! And that was the fellow from the country! The uneducated one who embarrassed him at his own meeting! What were they doing together? Why were they on the city wall? What was going on?

Quickly, he hid in the shadows. He thought to call the soldiers and have them arrested but then he might not find out what they were up to. He was straining his ear to hear but couldn't make out what they were saying. This...this was something! Something strange was going on in Despero that neither he nor Dolor were responsible for. Something terribly strange and curious.

They seemed to be parting and in the midst of saying farewell to each other. And then before his very eyes, the man seemed to disintegrate into dust and was blown away into the dark night by the soft wind!

Praeco wet his pants.

THE CITY OF DUBITO

Chapter One

"I can't believe it. It can't be true. How can Egenus be changed? An entire city?! How could they defeat troops from Elatus and Scelus?! They're a pathetic bunch, the whole lot of them."

"But they say that men from Lux overran the city. In droves they came and took Egenus by force."

"Do you believe it," another demanded.

"Of course not! But it makes good stories."

"Lux! Are you crazy man? There's no such place. Ancient fairy tales."

"So then what happened to Egenus then?"

"They changed their name. The name of the city."

"They changed it to Spes they say."

"Spes?!"

"What kind of name is Spes?"

"It's a stupid name, that's what it is."

"But how could they defeat troops from Elatus? I don't understand. Elatus has been kicking them around for as long as anyone knows. It has always been that way. Isn't that the way it should be?"

"And don't forget troops from Scelus. None left alive."

"But all that can't be true. It simply can't happen and never will."

"Aye."

"Aye."

"But do you think something could be happening?"

"Nah. The women were bored and got to making stories."

Prince Leo was sitting in the farthest, darkest corner of the bar yet he heard the conversation crystal clear, as if he had been sitting at the table with the men who were speaking across the room. He slowly sipped his malt beverage and listened, listened to the talk about what was or wasn't going on, what was or wasn't true. He was also waiting for someone.

"Would you like more sir," asked the barmaid.

"No. I'm quite fine thank you," Prince Leo replied to her.

She began to walk away but then stopped, turned and looked at him again. He saw her hesitation.

"Is there something wrong?" he asked her.

"No. I....no. Not at...you just happen to look...."

"...familiar?"

"Ye...yes. Familiar. Like I've seen you somewhere before."

"A dream perhaps," Prince Leo said turning his eyes away from hers.

"Exactly! A dream. How did you know?"

Prince Leo patiently finished his drink while the girl eyed him curiously.

"Who are you?" she finally asked.

Prince Leo took out money from his cloak and set it on the table. More than enough to pay for the drink. He rose from his chair and looked the girl in the eyes.

"Someone important."

He walked out of the bar to meet Misceo.

Misceo was excited. It had been eight moons ago since he left the land of Lux to come to this accursed place. Eight moons ago he left the side of Prince Leo in Sedes, the Crystal City, to blend into the lost throng inhabiting Nox, specifically Dubito for the past three. He had not wanted to leave the luminous glares of the City Sedes, the ever fragrant air and the piercing glory, for the land of perpetual darkness. A perpetual darkness that shall end when the King Unus stomps the ground of Nox, compelling it to give up Casus and his dispensable horde of filth.

Nevertheless, when Prince Leo had called him aside and begged his favor, to come and prepare for him, there was no way that he could refuse. It had baffled him, the mind of Leo and his father. Why not crush the wishful enemy? With less than a thought, the prince could accomplish it without any attention from the king. But this? All this toying? He could not understand. If the people of this land, which had once been Hortulus and was smiled upon by the king, decided out of some terrible mental illness, to embrace

Casus and his rabble, they too ought to be treated with impunity. But not King Unus. Not Prince Leo. They would hear nothing of it. They had a plan.

So he came here. Disguised as one of these. As a Noxian when in fact the design for his soul was forged in Sedes itself. He talked with them, like them, cooked and ate what they ate, brewed and drank what they drank, dressed and looked the way they did. But after all this time, he still wasn't any more like them at heart then when he first stepped out of the City of Sedes for Nox. Yes, he understood these people more, could sympathize more with their situation, but there was still that irreplaceable distance between he and they. Funny thing was, no one around him knew. For eight moons.

But tonight, he was about to meet Prince Leo after so long. It was hard to believe that all that time had passed since he had last seen his prince, more importantly, his friend. He remembered the long horseback rides that he and Prince Leo used to take through the crevasses of the Great Canyons of Otium. Sometimes they were accompanied by few of the lords of different lands but often, it was just the two of them. Prince Leo loved the canyons. He knew every detail of them down to the smallest pebble. A magical place. When they were there, the canyon seemed to breathe with its prince, inhale and exhale. The breeze was always light and gentle and ultimate serenity prevailed. The galloping and trotting sound of the hooves of their horses would echo musically of the natural walls and linger in the air.

Lux. A land of beautiful light.

"Misceo? Is that you?" inquired a squeaky, high pitched voice.

"Yeah. It's me."

"Misceo. Where are you going Misceo?"

Misceo stopped and turned around to face Insulus. He had known that it was Insulus even before turning around. That squeaky voice and the sound of his crutch on the cobblestone street always gave him away.

"Where am I going?"

"Yeah Misceo. Where are you going?"

What was he going to say? What was he going to do? He couldn't exactly tell him that he was on his way to meet Prince Leo of Lux, Son of King Unus, Lord of All Lands.

"I'm, uh, on my way to the Impietas to meet an old friend. Maybe have a drink."

"Why, can I come Misceo? Let me come with you. I've got money. I can buy a drink. Perhaps even one for you."

Misceo looked at Insulsus. He was a totally unimpressive man with a simple mind. He had no one and no one cared for him. Often he was treated horribly and with unwarranted disdain. He, Misceo, was one of the very few who treated this man with even a modicum of respect. Insulsus therefore, was quite fond of his company.

"Sure Insulsus. Come along."

"Thank you Misceo. Thank you."

They continued on to the Impietas. Misceo had to slacken his pace for Insulsus who had to contend with a wooden crutch for his bad left leg.

"Misceo?"

"Yes Insulsus?"

"Shall I meet your friend? The old friend you're going to meet?"

"Of course you can."

"Surely? You mean, you won't mind? I could go away when you meet your friend. Most people don't want me around much. I can get out of the way for when you meet your friend."

"No Insulsus. You'll meet my friend. He's a very nice person. You'll like him."

"Really?! Misceo, he's nice? Not many people like me Misceo. He might not like me. I'll get out of the way. I'll buy me a drink."

"No, no Insulsus. You'll have to meet my friend and I'm sure that he'll want to meet you."

Insulsus stopped.

"Meet me?"

Insulsus stood there staring at Misceo.

"Why would anyone want to meet me? No one's ever wanted to meet me before."

Misceo thought of what to say. What could he say?

"I can't understand why that is."

Leo?! It was Prince Leo's voice! Misceo was certain. It came from over there...there, someone leaning against the wall. In the dark, hooded robe.

"My lord?" Misceo uttered without thinking. His heart was racing and anxiety was overwhelming him.

Prince Leo lowered the hood from his head with a beaming smile all over his face.

"It's been long old friend," he said as Misceo ran up to him and embraced him.

Before Misceo knew it, tears were rolling down his face. As he touched Prince Leo, a flood of Lux came crashing down upon him. The scents, the sounds, the sights, the feel. It was more than he could bear. He had been longing for Sedes so deeply that he hadn't been able to acknowledge it. He had been here too long. He wanted...he needed home.

"You'll soon be going home Misceo," Prince Leo said to his weeping friend. "Soon, you'll be going home."

Misceo was embarrassed and tried to pull himself together.

"Aye. Soon."

"Well, shall I meet you Insulsus?" Prince Leo asked the dazed man.

Insulsus just stood there not knowing what to make of what he had just seen. Misceo called this man his lord, they were talking of going someplace else, home....

Misceo was attentive now and fumbled at an introduction.

"Uh.....," Misceo had forgotten Insulsus' name.

"Insulsus," Prince Leo offered.

"Yes. Yes of course," Misceo said further embarrassed. "Insulsus, this...uh...is...uh...."

"Leo. Prince Leo of Lux," Leo said extending his hand to Insulsus.

Misceo was stunned. Prince Leo just introduced himself to Insulsus as Prince Leo of Lux. He began to look around to see if anyone else was near enough to hear what had been said.

"Nice to meet you...prince?" Insulsus asked.

"Yes Insulsus."

Insulsus was confused. Prince? He hadn't heard of any prince? And of Lux? Lux sounded familiar but he didn't know much about it. Then he realized that Leo's hand was still extended and that he hadn't taken it.

"I'm sorry. Sorry. I apologize," he said firmly shaking Prince Leo's hand. "Prince you said? You're a prince?"

Misceo was getting nervous, very nervous.

"Actually, I am," Leo replied.

"I'm sorry. Just, I've never met one before. I don't know how to act. I'm sorry."

"Don't worry about it. It's perfectly fine Insulsus. Well, shall we go to your home Misceo?"

Misceo was totally engulfed in shock. He had been living here for so long, incognito, and Prince Leo just told Insulsus who he truly was and in public too.

"Sure. Yes. Definitely. Uh, right this way."

Misceo leading the way, the three turned around and started in the opposite direction. Insulsus couldn't stop staring at Prince Leo.

"May, may I ask you a question?"

"Sure. Anything Insulsus," Leo replied to him.

"Tell me about being a prince. What do you do? What are you doing here? Have you come to visit Misceo? He's very nice."

"I'm sure he's been nice to you," Prince Leo said looking at Misceo, "and about being a prince, I be myself and I do things like come here to Dubito."

"Oh."

Insulsus was thinking. Misceo kept looking around, hoping, praying that no one was eavesdropping or even within earshot.

"What do you do when you come here? Just visit Misceo? Why haven't I heard of you? Can't say others have heard of you, really. They don't say anything about a prince. At least, I haven't heard them."

"What's wrong with your leg Insulsus?" Prince Leo asked.

"Uh? My leg? It's fine. This leg is not too great," he said tapping his left leg. "That's why I use this stick, see. I use it and can go everywhere. Not a problem."

Prince Leo stopped.

"Why? What's wrong," Insulsus asked. "I can go anywhere, really. Just ask Misceo. I do this all the time and go anywhere I want to go. I've had this stick for...."

"Too long," Prince Leo asked.

"I don't know. Long time. But it's fine really. I'm used to it."

"Why don't you get rid of it?"

Insulsus was confused. He just told the prince that it was the stick that helped him get around. Perhaps Misceo's friend didn't want him to go with them.

"No, it's not that Insulsus. Just throw the stick down for a moment," Prince Leo responded out loud to his thoughts.

Insulsus looked at Misceo. What was going on?

"Throw it down for a minute Insulsus," Misceo said, reassuring him. "Trust me."

Insulsus eyed both of them suspiciously. He didn't know about this prince. He seemed nice until now. But Misceo he knew. Misceo had never hurt nor embarrassed him. He had often stood up for him when others were mocking and ridiculing him. Misceo might feel hurt if he didn't trust him now.

Slowly and staring at both Prince Leo and Misceo, Insulsus threw aside his crutch. He began to wobble and right when he was about to fall, Prince Leo stretched out his hand toward him and without touching him, lifted him into midair.

"How?! What? What's going on?! Put me down! Stop. Stop!" Insulsus said, terrified that he was in the air and his feet not touching the ground.

"This will only take a minute Insulsus," Prince Leo said. "Relax."

"What? What are you doing to me? What's that feeling in my leg? What are you doing?!"

Then slowly, Insulsus began to descend till his feet were resting on the ground.

"What?!"

Insulsus was standing, comfortably, and without his crutch. He had no pain in his joints. He wasn't wobbling. He lifted his left leg, flexed it, and stood back on it. He lifted his right leg, standing on his left leg alone and bounced on it. He didn't fall. He didn't have any pain.

He slowly looked up at Prince Leo and Misceo in bewilderment. His heart was pounding so hard he thought it might burst out of his chest. Prince Leo had his hands crossed upon his chest smiling. Misceo had tears in his eyes.

"I can stand," Insulsus said in a faint whisper. "I can stand up by myself.

I don't need my stick."

He looked back down at his legs. He did two squats. He looked back at the two men in front of him, one of them responsible for this...whatever it was.

He stood on one leg and then the other, back and forth. He jogged in place and was perfectly fine. He looked up at the two men again and slapped himself on both cheeks in order to rouse himself from any dream he might be having. No. He was awake alright.

Tears suddenly flooded his eyes. The expression on his face showed Prince Leo his complete gratitude more than any words could. Insulsus picked up his stick and ran screaming with joy into the night.

"My lord, the situation is deplorable. It is somewhat unbelievable that anyone could live like these poor people live. It is impossible for them to believe anything other than the things they can see and touch around them. To them, Lux is a figment of creative imagination and the king, an even farther stretch. Worse of all, perhaps, they deny the very existence of Casus. Since they see no enemy, how can they be delivered from that enemy? It's been difficult living here my lord."

Prince Leo was calmly and casually walking about the room examining the furniture Misceo had made. He had taken up the occupation of a carpenter and had proven quite good at it from what he, Leo, could see. And had done well for himself, comfortable, cozy home. Books. Many books.

"What do they read?" Prince Leo asked.

"Foolishness. They have scores and scores of writings on the preeminence of primary doubt. That's the religion, if any, that exists around here. All other systems of thought and science stems from that basic mind set."

Prince Leo ran his fingers down the spines of the books that stacked the bookcase along the wall. He closed his eyes and could feel the power and the lifeblood of this...ideology. He could taste its bitter cynical taste in his mouth. It was repulsive. Disgusting.

"My lord?"

Prince Leo was pulled back into the physical presence of his host.

"Yes Misceo."

"Insulsus. Why?"

"Why not, Misceo? Have you been away from Lux that long?"

"Nay, but.... It's just that I've been here, unknown, all this time and by that one act...."

"Misceo, you are not hiding. You were sent here to blend in with these people and learn of them and their perverted ways but not to hide from them or amongst them. What is there to hide from?"

"But I shan't be able to blend in anymore if you are discovered and I am found with you. What if Insulsus should say something?"

"And how will that injure me or my cause? You have performed admirably as I knew you would. You planted the words did you not?"

"Yes my lord."

"Good. There is nothing to worry about Misceo. I'll do what I want when I want. I could end all this now if I wanted but choose not to simply because my father and I have agreed not to. So if I choose to correct the physical wrong of Insulsus, I will. Anytime, place or way that I should choose."

"Forgive me, my...."

"Nothing to forgive Misceo."

Prince Leo smiled at his old friend.

"Are you well Misceo?"

"Aye my lord. Calloused," Misceo smiled in return looking down at his hands, "but well."

Prince Leo sat down at the table across from Misceo.

"So tell me about this city of yours."

"Very important. The river Pullus connects it to the very heart of Nox. It runs through the City of Magus, on through the center of Vitiosus, the central and largest city in Nox, and unto the fortress of Vorago, where we know Casus is. No one has journeyed there and returned to tell of it so no one here believes it even exists. But the river is the chief source of transportation and the basis of Dubito's economy."

"Economy based on?"

Misceo pointed to the bookshelf.

"Books, my lord. Books filled with rubbish they call wisdom. The whole economy here is based on the exporting of these books all over Nox. This city, it seems, is a city of learning. Great schools constitute this city and all people come from all over to study here. However, the greatest schools are in Vitiosus. So despite the fact that almost all the great books and texts are written here. Vitiosus...is still Vitiosus."

"And the authors of these books?"

"Some of them live here while most teach in Vitiosus. Those that live here are the ones with all the power and influence in this city. Their very word is law. Under them are the merchants who buy their books and sell them in the different cities, especially in Vitiosus. The City of Elatus comes close to Vitiosus in the purchase of this trash while Haeresis, deep in the south of Nox, is a close rival to the writing of books. Now the writings of Haeresis are most dangerous. Sometimes I think that they are the most dangerous literary executions that exist in the land."

Prince Leo sat in silence for awhile digesting Misceo's breakdown of the city's dynamic. He drummed his fingers on the surface of the table for a couple of beats and then stopped as abruptly as he had begun. Finally, he spoke.

"Interesting."

Chapter Two

Misceo awoke, startled, heart pounding, covered in blanket of sweat. The bed was moving, rocking violently! But it wasn't the bed. Something was covering the floor, waves of it! It was moving like water. But it looked like sand...mixed with fire...mixed with clouds....

Misceo screamed in stark terror. Ineffable fear rent at his soul. It was...this was Prince Leo's doing! It could only be. He knew for certain he was going to perish.

He couldn't look at it. He clutched the headboard of his bed and closed his eyes as tight as he could. He began to hear piercing shrieks from all over the city, sounding so distant compared to his own terror. What was the meaning of this? Was Prince Leo going to utterly destroy them all? Tears poured from his eyes. Never will he forget the awesome power of the prince and he would mediate on it till his fast approaching end arrived.

"Let go of the headboard."

It was Prince Leo! It was his voice. Misceo couldn't see him but he could hear him.

"I can't," Misceo cried. "I can't do it. I am going to perish. I'm finished."

Misceo felt like he could actually feel his heart pounding in his mouth, he was so afraid. He truly didn't want to take another breath with what was going on around him, his eyes firmly shut.

"Misceo?"

"M...my lord?"

"Let go."

It took every ounce of bravery Misceo had to begin to relax his fingers which held a vice grip on the finely done up wood. As terrified as he was, his terror was proof that Prince Leo was not to be disobeyed. Slowly his hold was undone and he was struggling to keep his balance on his rocking bed.

But then something else happened. He began to rise above his bed and float in the air. He opened his eyes and saw his bed swaying beneath him as if it were a raft upon an angry sea. It was actually adrift upon a steaming mixture of brown, blue, white and red. Blending into each other, burning and cooling into each other.

Prince Leo stood atop the highest pinnacle of the tallest and largest building in Dubito, the Lingua Printing Press. From there he could see and hear the entire city. People swimming and wading through the fluid mass while never failing to raise terrified voices pleading help and mercy. What was it that they believed around here, printed and taught the rest of their world, the rest of Nox? The preeminence of primary doubt. Ah! Why didn't they doubt this? And it was the authors and teachers of this doctrine who were screaming the loudest. He felt the eyes gazing up at him through tear matted lashes. The eyes of Dubito. They knew who he was. He needed no introduction. None of them had ever seen him before. None of them with the exception of Insulsus and Vates. Vates was the barmaid who served him while he was at the Impietas waiting for Misceo. She had actually seen him many times before, in her dreams. But even to the others in the city, he needed no introduction. In their hearts, Dubito knew who he was, where he was from, why he was here... and what was to come. The sight of him awakened hidden, forgotten visions of the soul, put things in their proper perspective.

"Come to me, Misceo," Prince Leo said. His voice so casual as if Misceo was but a few feet away from him.

He heard Prince Leo's voice and began to feel himself turn in the air toward the open window. As he sailed through it and up over the panicked city, he could hardly believe his eyes. Dubito was flooded with that.... It looked and acted like water, but you knew it was sand, then you knew it was fire but then again you could see the clouds in it. What sort of madness was this? What manner of unfathomable power could produce such atrocity of nature? Yet, the whole thing looked perfectly natural and flowed and coexisted as if those elements were in their proper state!

The screams, however, were unbearable. Fear was in the air so strong you could taste it. Men, women and children swam or tried to swim to safety atop buildings and in trees. Misceo wondered how it felt, that fluid substance. Did it burn? Was it cold? Frigid or felt like quicksand? He would never know. Wasn't so sure he really wanted to know.

He turned to see Prince Leo standing atop the Lingua Printing Press. Prince Leo's back was turned to him but he knew Prince Leo knew he was there.

Misceo looked down and couldn't stop himself from trembling.

"Are you ready to leave Misceo?"

Misceo's teeth were chattering.

"Yes.... Yes my lord. Whenever you choose."

Besides, he didn't feel as though he was in the position to argue. Prince Leo's power held him a great distance, high up in the air.

"Misceo," Prince Leo said with his back still facing him.

"My lord?"

"I am grateful for your work here. I shan't ever forget."

"I aim only to serve you and your father the king."

"Greet him for me, Misceo. Tell him all is well."

Misceo thought he heard a quiver in Prince Leo's voice. But then again, so high up, he didn't trust his senses.

"I shall my lord."

"I'll see you soon old friend...."

Misceo was shot away almost as if at the very speed of light. Before he could think his next thought, he had stopped. When he opened his eyes, he realized that he was no longer in the land of Nox.

Vates couldn't join in the symphony of screams. She was choking on the intense fear that formed a lump in her throat. Her skin was searing in this fluid inferno as it burned, froze, sanded and cooled her body, all simultaneously.

The horror was just more than her vocal organs could express in any manner of sound. This was a nightmare. Strangely, a nightmare she had seen before. A nightmare she had prayed would stay in her dreams. But it was present in the here and now. She was in pain. Her heart was in a state of shock. Her brain was in panic.

Through her agony, for some unknown reason, she lifted her head and looked up. There was a man atop the Lingua building. He was calm and collected. He wasn't frightened like the rest of them. He...was familiar. He was looking straight at her.

Who was this man? Where was he from? What was he doing here? It was him! He was...doing this? But how? This had to be a dream? How was this possible? But for sure she knew the pain was real, her fear was more real than anything she could have experienced. That man was real. That very man she had seen before in her dreams. This very day. This very sadness. This very horror. This very fear. This very same revelation.

The sound of pain finally broke free and rang through Vates' voice and filled the air around her.

Chapter Three

Sleep. He made them sleep. They had been through a long and tough ordeal. They needed the rest.

Prince Leo gave them the deepest, best sleep they had ever had. Rest to the mind, body and spirit. Complete rest. He hadn't enjoyed what he did but that's the way he chose to deal with Dubito and his method would yield precisely the kind of results he wanted.

"What are you going to do," asked the voice. "Why are you letting them sleep?"

The liquid mass began to rescind onto the Lingua Printing Press and climb up to where Prince Leo was standing. It instantly dissolved upon touching his feet.

"Why are you putting them to sleep? You want them to believe in you and your precious father and after that show, you put them to sleep?! They're obviously going to think it was all a dream. You just nullified everything you just did! Have you lost your...."

"You will mind your tongue Casus," Prince Leo coolly responded.

Silence. Only the sizzling sound of the fluid mass dissolving at Prince Leo's feet.

"Tell me what you're up to."

"And why should I?"

"You're going to do whatever you want to do anyway. You might as well give me some room to maneuver. Tell me what's going on!"

"Your problem, Casus, is that you are too emotional. You allow your emotions to blind your judgement. Isn't it obvious that I am giving you room to maneuver?"

Silence.

"So now you see?"

"Yes. Yes, I see. I'll have you know that I hate both you and I hate your father! And very, very much so! You both with your arrogant, conceited ways! You are both sick! Disgusting! You show me no respect whatsoever! Is it any wonder I led a rebellion against your rule? I swear I hate you! Both of you are going to regret this. I promise. At the very first opportunity, I will destroy every sniveling maggot in the land of Nox! I am going to...."

"Be gone Casus. Till later."

A soft, gentle breeze floated in over the City of Dubito, brushing smoothly against Prince Leo as he looked out over the city. There was, now, no sign of the liquid, elemental mixture that had just recently been all over the city and choking the life out of it. But there were bodies of people everywhere, cradled in the arms of slumber. A tear formed in Prince Leo's left eye and trickled down his face. Some part of him wanted them to never wake up to the world around them, not this one. He would definitely wish them awake to the brilliant, vibrant life and light of Lux, but that couldn't happen. Not now.

He looked over them as a father looks over his sleeping children. This was all that he wished them, peace.

Pure, unadulterated peace. Sublime wisps of the coolest, clearest breeze entering their nostrils and permeating their souls. That's what they all deserved and that's what he wanted so desperately to give...and more.

But for now, sleep. Only sleep, but sorely needed. And when they awoke, questions, confusion and doubt awaited them. Casus was sure to deliver the very best he could to erase any memory of his entire visit here in Dubito. Obliterate any notion that this day ever came to pass.

Prince Leo's feet slowly lifted off the roof of the Lingua Printing Press building. The movement was so natural that it seemed as if anyone could do it. The air seemed to pick him up and embrace him into itself. As if it longed for him. As if it yearned for him.

Prince Leo thought about the City of Dubito and it's people. Some would try to forget but others would remember. Forever.

THE CITY OF MAGUS

"He's coming. I can feel him coming."

"Yes, yes. But how? How is the question. He can be felt in the ground, the wind, the trees."

"Shhh! Be quiet. It's all of them you fool. He's in everything."

"How is that possible? Lord Casus is the only one who can do that. It says so in the Artificium Niger. I've studied the texts thoroughly."

"Shhh! You ask too many questions."

"What should we do?"

"Go back and alert the Veneficus. That was all we were sent here to do. Let him dare come to Magus. They will tear him apart!"

Where two bodies crouched behind the bushes, two snakes now slithered away. But eyes watched them from the ground below, the trees around and the night sky above.

Chapter One

The two entered the gates of the valley city in human form. It was night and it was always unusually dark in Magus. That's how its citizens liked it and the only way the Veneficus would have it.

The Veneficus. Now they were something to fear. For him, they terrified him. Alumno had been a student of the Artificium Niger since he was a toddler and showed great promise. He was a prodigy. Mastering complex incantations and ecstatic meditative consciousness with astounding speed. He had been blessed as a tender child with revelations of Lord Casus the Majestic himself. By the time he had seen six moons, he had been pulled out of the common schools and was under tutelage at the Refectorium ex Astrum, the same building that housed the Veneficus. He lived and studied there for twelve moons before he finally met them. And that day was the saddest and most terrible day of his life.

He remembered his initial excitement however. Being that most activity of any real significance in Magus took place at night, he was instructed to get enough rest that day. Usually, he was more than eager to obey orders. It was his goal to be the best medicus in Magus, in Nox. He dreamed of someday going to the fabled City of Vorago and of being a special aide to Lord Casus himself. His earlier aspirations had been to become a member of the Veneficus. But when he learned that such a dream was impossible, he put it aside. The Veneficus took no members and they lost no members. They were the Veneficus. The most powerful force ever, second only to the mystical Lord Casus the Majestic and perhaps the Imperators.

So how could he sleep? How could he rest or relax? He, Alumno was about to meet them. Who knew? Perhaps they would be so impressed with him that they might change their mind about a new member. They knew everything about him and his progress. They must know that he was the youngest scholar of the Artificium Niger. He could, on the spur of a moment, recite and translate The Thousand and One Mystical Voices of Lord Casus and could perform some of the most complex incantations without audibly uttering a single word. Though hardly anyone in the Refectorium ex Astrum would admit it, he knew he dazzled them and forced upon all the other medicum nothing short of stark envy.

The time finally came. The dead of night. He left his private quarters and proceeded to the general hall, passing through the walls of the Refectorium ex Astrum. There were no doors in the entire building. If you were within its walls, that meant that you were a skilled medicus and therefore you would have no use for doors. He arrived in the general hall to find two of his instructors. These two, he didn't even know their names. It had not ceased to shock him how very impersonal everyone was in the Refectorium. No one knew anyone, really, and didn't care to. It was because everyone was in competition with everyone else. One medicus might kill a rival or weaker medicus at any time. For this reason, everyone kept on their toes, practiced and studied hard and always watched their back. Making a friend was deadly and therefore unheard of. No one cared about anyone. It was a very cold and lonely place.

His instructors didn't say anything. No word of congratulations or encouragements. Actually, they seemed to scowl at him. Most likely, they themselves had never had the opportunity to meet the Veneficus. One of them gave him a black candle. He already knew that he was to light it when he got there. The other one drew a circle on the floor around him with some white chalk and then they left the hall. Now, the general hall was at ground level with the outside of the building. So one could say that it was the first floor of the sixty that went up into the sky in pyramid form to the Corona, the top suite. The Veneficus, according to what he had been told, had never stepped foot on any of these floors. They were deep beneath the Refectorium, very deep.

Despite the dense mental fog of his nervousness, he knew what he had to do and realized that it was time to do it. He took a deep breath, closed his eyes and began to speak in an arcane tongue. Soon, he felt the floor give and his body began to descend.

Thoughts began to bombard his mind. Where was he going? How far down was it? What would he find? What would they look like? Above him lay probably the most splendid building in all of Nox. The Refectorium was adorned in gold, silver, amethyst, bronze, sapphire, diamonds, emeralds, marble floors, cedar wood...everything there was the best. Of course he imagined the unseen city of Lord Casus would be by far more splendid, but the dwelling of the Veneficus? He could only imagine!

Alumno's feet hit solid ground with a splash and he buckled over and vomited so hard tears dripped from his eyes. He felt an instant, considerable decline in his health. He had never inhaled such foul odor ever before in his life! It was so strong, the stench, that he struggled to stay on his feet in the pitch black darkness. After several minutes of trying desperately to gather himself together, he lit the black candle in his hand with only a word.

Startled, he almost dropped it. There was a child standing right before him and looking at him in the face as if he were silly. It was a little boy who could not be a day over six moons. He was standing there filthy and naked.

What was a child doing here? How did he get here?

Alumno bent the light of the candle over to the floor and realized that the floor was covered with blood about two to three inches deep all around, his vomit floating about his feet. He returned his attention to the boy, who now, wasn't there.

Had he been hallucinating? Had there indeed been a child standing before him? Where did he go? Why weren't there any ripples in the blood covering the floor if he had turned and ran? Could he possibly be a servant of the Veneficus or even one of them?

The stench was unbearable and Alumno felt himself getting dizzy. What could cause such odor? Tears flowed from his eyes and he could feel himself getting ill again. He was struggling to stand. He bent over, using an incantation to balance the candle by itself in midair, rested his hands on his knees and vomited again. He was filled with disgust as he watched his vomit float on the stale, thick blood carpet. He spat to get the remnants of it out of his mouth and when he looked up to grab the candle, another child was holding it in one hand and sucking on a human bone with the other. He stepped back in horror and bumped into an old man with a long dirty beard.

Alumno was scared and felt his heart beat accelerating to dangerous levels. He squinted and could now see two other kids, three men and three women. One of the men was very old while the other two were young and attractive. Of the women, two were old and the other seemed middle aged. The Veneficus. These were the Veneficus and he now had no desire, whatsoever, to be one of them or even around them. They were the cause of the stench that had to be far beyond repulsive. One of the young men stepped forward and, with a wave of his hand, a force brought Alumno before him. He looked Alumno over and with his long index fingernail, cut into Alumno's cheek. He rubbed his finger in the cut and offered his bloody finger to one of the old hags who tasted the blood. She stood there pondering for a moment and then finally said, "Ten more."

They all turned away from him and began to move into the darkness with the exception of one of the children. A little girl offered him a human hand. Alumno cringed backwards in shock, inciting laughter from the child who scurried away gleefully. Pain pierced his petrified heart. He had recognized the ring on the hand.

The people cleared the streets before them. They were the elite. The most powerful medicum in the land. They were the inhabitants of the Refectorium ex Astrum and they were distinguished by the aura they carried around with them. This was the part of the whole thing that Alumno loved most. This was just one of the many perks of being a scholar of the Artificum Niger, the ultimate book of the Ars.

They proceeded regally through the streets; dignified and with all the pomp worthy of their station. Out of the corner of his eye, Alumno could see and sense the awe that was being sprayed his way. And by both old and young. He had seen only twenty-four moons old and was one of the most powerful medicus in the entire land of Nox.

His companion stopped.

"What? What is it," Alumno asked.

He didn't respond but kept looking forward. Alumno felt it before he saw. He looked ahead and saw a hooded figure in the middle of the street in front of them. For some unexplained reason, his heart sank. Was this the one?

His companion, began to murmur incantations and began running full speed toward the figure. He knew he ought to assist him in the attack but for some reason, he didn't. He was more curious about what would happen then in participating. So instead, he uttered phrases of invisibility and instantly became undetectable to the human eye.

He had spent forty of his forty-three moons in the Refectorium. He had learned. He had mastered. And yet, he had never met the Veneficus. He was never blessed with a vision of Lord Casus the Majestic. Not once! But this child?! Why? What was wrong with him, Invidere? What was wrong with the sacrifices he had made? What was lacking in his dedication, his devotion to the study of the Ars?

But that was okay. He would rectify it all today. He, Invidere, now had a golden opportunity presented to him. Lord Casus was giving him a chance to prove himself for what he knew he deserved, the glory, the honor. He will destroy this intruder who had been causing panic in the scared realms. Things have never been the same since this filth stepped foot in Nox. There had been countless glitches in incantations and realmic disruptions. Almost every one of the medicum in the Refectorium complained of ill visions, that were filled with blasphemies and abominations. Things like Lord Casus bowing down to someone else and scenes of him being humiliated and destroyed. Nightmares of the destruction that took place outside the walls of Egenus, chaos in Despero and ghastly liquid flooding Dubito even before these things had actually happened. No bother. He will die today at the learned skill of Invidere.

As he approached the hooded figure, he called for a sword to materialize in his hand. It did. As he reached the man and swung, something happened that he had never seen, felt nor heard of before. The ground below him pulled back leaving his swing sufficiently out of reach. The shock and movement combined caused him to lose his balance. He fell flat on his bottom. Sitting there embarrassed, he turned his head to both sides of the street and saw the people staring in amazement. They were staring at the abasement of one of their venerable leaders.

Enraged, Invidere determined to put all of his skill to work. From the seated position on his rear end, he shot straight up in the air and hovered above the ground. Above ground because he didn't trust it anymore. It obviously wasn't on his side. He stood there fuming and glaring at his opponent. Who was he and what exactly was he doing here? He hated the man like he had never hated anyone before.

The stranger slowly lowered the hood off his head and looked Invidere in the eye.

"My name is Leo."

With a snap of his fingers, Invidere summoned two gigantic fire balls, one in each hand.

"It makes no difference to me what your name is," Invidere snarled.

He clapped his hands together, sandwiching Prince Leo and bringing the fireballs to a thunderous explosion on either side of him. The detonation filled the street with fire, incinerating three bystanders on the spot. Invidere smiled and waited patiently for the smoke and dust to settle. He would scoop up the pile of ashes, if there were any, and keep it in a golden urn. His trophy. A symbol of his power, learning and skill. He would thus, validly, declare himself the most prominent medicus of all.

"It ought to matter to you what my name is Invidere."

What?! It was the voice of the man. The flames and smoke slowly began to dissipate and a form stood standing in the midst of it. Nothing, no one could withstand that! Nothing could survive that! But there he stood as everything settled, staring at him unflinching and unscathed.

His voice was calm. Not emotional. He clearly wasn't the least bit afraid nor intimidated. Invidere heard the sounds of a new kind of awe sweeping the crowd. It wasn't awe at him or what he could do, but rather awe of this stranger and his apparent might. Now, Invidere was getting concerned. Perhaps this wasn't such a good idea. Attacking a strange foe without knowing anything about him. And in full view of the people. But it was too late now.

"Think Invidere! Think!" he thought to himself. "This arrogant fool is standing here begging you, daring you to try to kill him, or even hurt him. You have to do something and quick."

He stretched out his hand to the sword laying on the ground a few feet away and it came flying into his hands. He tried to thrust it into Prince Leo's heart but within a foot of Leo the steel blade crumbled up as if not wanting to have anything to do with this killing. The Leo fellow didn't flinch, didn't shudder or turn. He just stood there looking at him.

There was only one thing that was coming to mind. The most dangerous incantation he knew. Summoning the Hordes of Casus. To perform it with the most safety, it required at least three powerful medicum. Three people. Their strength, their energy, all their concentration and every ounce of their skill. However, if he could pull it off, his new friend here would be reduced to nothing more than a five day old heap of maggot infested rotting flesh.

Invidere formed his fingers into the shape of a five pointed star and released unnatural sounds from deep down within himself.

The Hordes of Casus?! The fool!

Alumno was shaking. He looked at the people on either side of the street watching the spectacle and felt a sharp panic. They had no idea. The Hordes of Casus was arguably the most powerful, destructive and exhausting incantation ever, designed for nothing other than complete annihilation. According to the Artificium Niger, there was a vassal long ago who sought to overthrow Lord Casus. His name was Unus. He was mighty and powerful and with great cunning he designed to destroy Casus the Majestic and rule supreme over Nox and with an iron hand. He had nearly been successful when Lord Casus forged from the blood of his own wounds the incantation known as the Hordes of Casus. This incantation drew together the energy from every ancient warrior under Casus and released a power unheard of. It was this incantation that forced Unus into retreat to distant caves in the abyss where he is even now slowly dying of his wounds inflicted at the hands of Lord Casus. The conjuring of this amazing force is studied in the Refectorium for historical purposes only and even that, with great care. No one in Nox who is not an inhabitant or has never once studied in the Refectorium knows of this legendary power. It is and has been, taboo to even speak of it. But here, now, in the public streets of Magus, this idiot seeks to employ its power against some bizarre, rogue medicus?

Still cloaked in invisibility, Alumno ran for cover. He could only hope that some providence would save him and these people from the pending disaster.

Invidere felt himself fading away. He could feel the blood cells struggling in his veins to circulate through his body. His vision was waning in and out and his mind felt like sharp pins were piercing his consciousness. He was sweating profusely and the taste of his own blood began to fill his mouth. He tried to gulp it down but didn't have the strength. It seeped out of the sides of his mouth. But whatever happened to him, he wasn't going to give up.

He kept on conjuring and conjuring. Arms trembling and urine spilling down his legs. That same instant he defecated himself thrice and his eyes began rolling up into his head. He felt the bone in his right thigh snap and tears raced down his face. Yet he kept on and on.

Black sulphurous smoke began to fill the air around Invidere and Prince Leo and soon became caustic. A fresh wave of darkness swept over them and began to boil over. Prince Leo just stood there unfazed.

Invidere thought he felt a crack in his skull. He was going to die. He knew it. The tears pouring down his face were now red and so was the sweat tearing its way through his skin. The bones in his left arm and two of his ribs all snapped at once and he knew he wouldn't be able to complete the incantation as his teeth started to pop out of their sockets and he struggled not to swallow them.

Nine figures. Hovering around. Three children. Three men. Three women. Some elderly. Hovering around. Holding on to his strength. Helping him...complete the...Hordes....

Alumno looked as black smoke whirled around in the air in serpentine wisps. But...something. Familiar. A horrible presence, stench, that he knew all too well and would never forget. The Veneficus! They were here.

Alumno tried to see but his eyes fell to the ground in pain as they burned in their sockets. They were helping that fool complete the incantation! But here in the street? Could there be anywhere more unsafe and dangerous? Did they want this person destroyed that bad? Bad enough to help an idiot? The Veneficus?

A wave of power, almost like the tail of some great beast, picked Alumno up and slammed him against a building. It was so dark he couldn't see. There was blood at the corner of his mouth and terror was squeezing the life out of him. He heard people screaming all around him as the ground began to shake violently. Eerie sounds shouted rhythms of fear and huge foot stomps could be heard everywhere as mammoth phantoms, terrifying to the soul began to materialize and step out of the intense blackness.

"Enough."

Uh? Wha.... Everything sto...pped.... Why....

Invidere was on his knees on the ground before Prince Leo and in his final seconds. He heard Prince Leo and saw the effect of his one word. He saw Prince Leo's eyes looking at him in pity. As if his every effort was nothing but vain, naught. As harmless as a kitten's purr. He wanted to hate him one last time but he had nothing left as he surrendered to the final throb of his already semi-solid, decaying heart.

What?! How? How?!

Alumno licked at the blood in the corner of his mouth and spat it out. He breathed the air and it was clear, despite the usual stink of incense and mystical potions designed to enhance sight into the scared realm.

How?!

He rubbed his eyes and looked in the direction of his companion and the stranger. His fellow colleague from the Refectorium lay in a heap while the stranger stood there totally unharmed! What kind of power was this? How could this be possible? How could he withstand the most powerful incantation of all time, not to mention the power of the Veneficus? This simply could not be possible!

Leo? Did he hear the stranger say that his name was Leo? Is that what he told his colleague?

Wait. He was walking. He was headed in his direction. He tried to look at his body to make sure he was still invisible. He couldn't see his own hand raised before his face. He couldn't see his feet or the rest of his body. Yet, this Leo, was looking straight at him and was coming towards him. He wanted to run but was afraid to. He didn't know what Leo might do.

"That's Prince Leo to you," the stranger said. "Take me to the Refectorium."

As Leo's words floated in Alumno's direction, he became visible again. It were as though nothing could be hidden from him or his words. He stood there spellbound staring at Prince Leo. The awesomeness within his command and the sheer power that radiated from him. A purity that made him feel ashamed of himself and his life.

"Now," Prince Leo commanded.

"Ye-es, my lord?" Alumno managed to say, getting up off the ground and on his feet.

"Much better. To the Refectorium."

They had entered the city with all the prestige they had been accustomed to. Now he was the hostage of a strange medicus who commanded terrible power. In fact, the entire city was now being held hostage by this great medicus.

What would Lord Casus think of this? What if he found out about this? What would happen? What would become of them all? He had never really heard of any power truly greater than that of Lord Casus. Could this be some distant relative of his? Or, was this Unus escaped from the abysmal dungeon?

Alumno tried to steal a look at Prince Leo but was afraid to do so. He felt overwhelmed by his presence. No, no. This wasn't Unus. He said he was Prince Leo. He, then, must be prince of some distant land. Son of a king. Perhaps the old fables were true. Of a distant land of light and beauty where life was all bliss. But then why come here? Was this a conquest? But no army? Well, then again, with power like that, who needs an army?

Alumno was scared.

They were soon at the huge, black stone walls of the Refectorium. This is where all medicum paused to employ their skill in the Ars and reduced their human density in order to pass through the thick walls, six feet thick.

Prince Leo kept on walking. He didn't even break stride.

Prince Leo was about a foot away from the wall when something happened that Alumno had never seen happen before. He had never ever even heard of it happening. The stones of the wall dispersed into dust before him and remained suspended in the air, though out of his way so that he had a clear, clean path into the building.

Prince Leo kept on walking without pause.

Alumno's heart was pounding. What was this? What was this power? This strength and confidence? Where was this man from? Where did he study? Under whom did he learn? Was this power the Ars or some other, higher, more effective discipline and how could he master it so? This man seemed young but wielded in his eyes a gaze produced only through ancient wisdom. How old was he?

"Are you coming," he heard Prince Leo's voice say to him from within the building.

He entered hastily after him. But when Alumno entered the general hall, what he saw almost made him faint. The shock was overpowering. There, on their knees, was the Veneficus, behind them, every medicus in the Refectorium! Everyone on their knees before this Prince Leo!

Prince Leo stood there for a moment looking at the spectacle. Alumno had a feeling that he was dissatisfied with it. For the first time, Alumno noticed the fragrant aroma that accompanied Prince Leo. It was subtle yet powerful. Airy and sublime. Potent enough though to totally purge the air of the foul stench of the great Veneficus.

"Alumno, lead me to the Corona," Prince Leo said without turning to look at him.

One of the Veneficus, one of the younger men, glared at Alumno as if to say, "Hurry! What are you waiting for?!"

"Yes, my lord," Alumno said to Prince Leo and began to ascend in the air, up over the general hall and through the floors of the Refectorium.

"The Corona," Alumno thought to himself. The Corona was the highest and most luxurious suite in the entire, gigantic Refectorium ex Astrum! So he had heard, at least. He had never been there. It was where Lord Casus was said to have stayed whenever he came to the City of Magus. The Corona itself was like another dimension, he heard, of power, splendor and glory. From the stories he had heard, he doubted if he would manage to remain alive to reach the Corona, much less lead Prince Leo there. Great Imperators of Lord Casus' host resided in the floors and rooms leading to the Corona. These were generals who had fought in the ancient wars against Unus and were bathed in might. Those floors were strictly prohibited from any and every medicus.

But, as they ascended, every floor looked deserted. Every floor was deserted! Every floor. Where were they? There were signs of hasty departure and though he had never seen them, he himself had often felt their heavy presence. But right now, absent. Gone. Fle.... Wait a minute. They fled! They fled the building! They knew he was in the city and fled! Maybe, they could feel Prince Leo's approach. They probably fled the entire city. The only other beings left in the building were the ones on their knees in the general hall paying homage to Prince Leo! Could this get anymore bizarre? Everything he had learned and studied these past twenty-two moons seemed to be crumbling down around him. He was having a sneaking suspicion that he had been lied to.

Before he knew it, a strong hand grabbed him and was carrying him. It was Prince Leo. The intensity of the power that high up in the Refectorium had been affecting and making him dizzy, though he hadn't realized it. He would have fallen a couple of stories before his incantation wore off and he would have slammed into one of the floors below with a crash. Death.

Prince Leo held him by the hand and carried him.

Chapter Two

Prince Leo looked around the room. It was better than his most recent accommodations in Nox, though very modest compared to what he was used to in Lux. And he was hungry. He turned to Alumno.

"I want some dinner. Bring me up something."

Alumno was groggy and felt like he was about to pass out. His body wasn't used to all this, glory or intensity or whatever it was. He had never been this high up in the Refectorium before.

"Uh, my lord.... I don't think I'll be able to make it."

"Don't worry. You will cause I send you."

"Y-es my lord."

Alumno descended through the floor.

"Casus, your little set up here is pathetic," Prince Leo said into the air.

"It works though, doesn't it. I am king here. I am god here. These people all worship me. They obey me and not your precious father. Isn't that enough? Isn't that enough proof?"

"Proof of what?"

"Proof tha...."

"Enough Casus. Later."

Silence ensued.

Prince Leo flopped down in a golden chair covered with a thick, black velvet cloth by the window and gazed down at the city below. His thoughts were on the pile of flesh and bones matted with blood and crawling with maggots still lying in the city street. The remnants of a man once called Invidere. Invidere was a man who had never known peace. He had never known rest. He had never, truly just sat back and laughed a full hearted laugh. Had never smiled a sincere smile from the soul. Worse yet, he had died desperately trying to hate he, Leo, with his very last heartbeat. And Invidere hadn't even known who it was that he was trying so much to hate with every ounce of his last strength.

Sad. This whole place was sad. He probably ought to level this whole building with everyone in it. Make sure no one else studies this foolishness. These stupid little dog tricks Casus teaches these people to deceive them into thinking they're powerful. He, Casus, had them wrapped so tight in a deadly circle of lies and illusions that they couldn't even see the senselessness of it all. They couldn't even think. Couldn't utilize their most basic reasoning abilities. The whole thing made him sick!

Alumno began to recover as he approached the lower levels of the Refectorium. However, he was very exhausted and mentally depleted. The lower levels were busy and filled with whispers. Everyone eyed him curiously and with some tints of envy. He was much too spent, however, to appreciate all the attention though. Plus, fear kept pounding and stabbing at him.

When he finally reached the general hall, a medicus was waiting for him by a chalk drawn circle on the floor. As he had guessed, the Veneficus wanted to see him.

By the time he arrived to the lowest levels inhabited by the Veneficus and was punched in the face by the foul, pungent odors there, debilitation subdued him and he splashed down in the stale, shallow pool of blood that covered the floor.

"On your feet!!"

It was a sharp female voice. One of the older ones. He was soon surrounded by all nine of them, glaring at him as if everything that had happened was somehow his fault.

He managed to pull himself up.

"Where is Invidere," a very young voice demanded. One of the children. A boy.

"Invidere?" Alumno didn't understand the question.

"Yes Invidere! Where is he?"

"He's dead."

"What do you mean he's dead?" asked another voice.

What was this, Alumno thought to himself. They knew just as well as he did what had happened to him. They were there! He felt their presence. They helped Invidere complete the Hordes of Casus. They saw what happened. They saw how Prince Leo disrupted everything. They were trying to kill him and failed. Why were they acting as if they didn't know what had happened? Acting as if they never left the building?

"He died trying to invoke the Hordes of Casus against Prince Leo in the street."

They were looking at each other as though they were surprised. Were these people for real? They had failed to kill Prince Leo and were now trying to save face, distance themselves from the embarrassment.

He began to wonder, why were they still here? Why were they still in the Refectorium? Why hadn't they fled the city like the Imperators had? From the way they were acting, he knew that they would have jumped ship at the very first opportunity. Did Lord Casus make them stay?

"Did it work?"

The little girl was now asking the question.

"Did what work?"

"The Hordes of Casus, you fool! Did it work?"

He had just about had it with these stupid questions. He was exhausted and didn't have the energy to play their little game.

"Weren't you all there?"

Alumno let out a scream that could freeze time. It was as if nine needles pierced his heart all at once and from every angle. He collapsed in a heap.

"Never, ever, forget your place!"

One voice. But the voice of all nine. Yet one distinct voice. Alumno wanted to just die and have today over with.

"We ask the questions!"

The voice of one of the young men.

"You give the answers!"

The voice of the younger lady.

Alumno knew that he would never forget that for the rest of his mortal life.

"You will be the host for our guest, but don't ever forget in whose hand your life rests."

"Do NOT speak to him!"

"Only speak when spoken to."

"Know that he lies. Everything he says is a lie."

"Pay his lies no heed."

"Did he say anything to you in the Corona?"

"Yes my lords," Alumno's voice cracked with fear.

"Well? What did he say?"demanded the little girl.

"He said to take him some dinner."

Baffled, as if he had spoken in some other language, they stared at each other as if confused. He had thrown them off and they were trying to make sense of what he had just said. One of them finally spoke up.

"Then what are you still doing here! Hurry! Make sure the best...."

"...the very best is prepared!"

"And with the utmost care!"

"And with the utmost haste!"

He instantly found himself lying on the floor of the general hall, confused and racked with pain. The general hall? They must have shot him up here. Apparently, he was learning who jumped when who spoke.

There were a lot of things on Prince Leo's mind. The people of Nox for one. All the people he had met. All the people who were now involved in this so called "rebellion" of his. Rebellion when in a blink of an eye he could make everything right, fix every wrong. This process was slow, taxing but probably best in the long run. It did make for something to do. Made for a good story. Most of all, however, the personal way he touched the lives of these people was worth it. That he had to admit.

Lately he had found himself doused in melancholy. Just look at this world around him. Nothing short of pitiful. He looked down at the city below and at those poor people who practiced and studied Casus' little bag of tricks. And what was worse, they looked up to the fools here in the Refectorium who worshiped Casus the Idiot. Those people down there who were often poor and hungry and looking for some fulfilment in their lives. All their attempts and sacrifices proved futile. Some lived out their lives, earnest in that quest, and died without ever realizing it.

The children. Prince Leo thought of the children. The babies being born. The innocents that came into this world and life of no choice of their own, oblivious to what lay ahead of them. As they grew, they got to understand the nature of this reality and adjusted themselves accordingly. Deal with hunger, deal with thirst, deal with unmet needs, cold, nakedness and the frustration of not being afforded the necessary opportunities to reach one's ultimate potential. These things, to them, were part of life. They were accepted without question. Without a second guess or doubt.

The kids grew up into young men and women, had babies of their own, taught them this philosophy of life and expected them to embrace it from the cradle. Teaching the world view that rightly ought to be called the Struggle of Futility. Eventually they grow old, their bodies slow down, become weaker, the light in their eyes grow dim and they look back over their lives and are thankful for one thing and one thing only. They're thankful, not that they lived life, but that they survived it as long as they did.

A tear rolled down Prince Leo's face. He longed for the coming future.

Alumno struggled to his feet. He knew that if he didn't get up and moving, not only would the Veneficus be upset with him, but Prince Leo would also be irritated. And that was more terrifying than the former. He had seen first hand, the abilities of this Prince Leo and how he so easily put the terrifying Veneficus on edge. He was caught between these two powers that were obviously at odds with each other. He felt like a pawn in a deadly game.

He stood and staggered. He murmured incantations and gathering strength, managed to make it to the extremely, large kitchen. He gave the order and accented it by mentioning the strange, mysterious Prince Leo who they all greeted in the general hall and the Veneficus. The mentions, he was sure, would ensue haste and the best skill.

He sank into a chair as he waited, thinking over the night's events. A powerful medicus actually died tonight. Although he hadn't known Invidere by name until Prince Leo mentioned it.... How did he know Invidere's name anyway? But then again, that was probably the very least of the day's surprises. Tonight, for the first time ever, he saw the seemingly infinitely large general hall filled to capacity. No one knew for sure, exactly how many people resided in the Refectorium but today he saw them all. Everyone was kept apart. They hardly ever knew each other by name and for the most part, they all pretty much hated each other. It was competitive. Everyone was trying to outdo everyone else to be better, the most powerful. Sometimes, he longed for a friend, someone to talk to. But that in itself was a sign of weakness that any medicus in the Refectorium would seek to exploit to his or her advantage. Many unfortunates had learned that the hard way.

But he did have a friend once. An older man who had lived in the Refectorium almost his entire life. Alumno was just a little boy entering the Refectorium for the first time and was scared. He had never really been away from his mother before and, though was fascinated by everything he saw and was learning, he missed home, he missed his mother. He had been her only child and from the look of things, they were never going to see each other again. Medicus within the Refectorium didn't socialize with those outside, not even those in the city. Every now and then, a few medicum would be allowed to go to certain houses were there would be women available. That however, was the most outside contact they had.

The man's name was Turbatus, one of the most powerful medicus Alumno had ever known. Turbatus knew everything. He could recite incantations without hardly thinking about them, they just flowed out of him. Everything he did, and all the skills he had accumulated had become second nature to him. It was almost as if he was born with all the knowledge of the Artificium Niger in his head. He knew everything in the scared book like the back of his hand. No one would have dared challenge him; he was so powerful. He had an exceptional mind and Alumno only dreamed of being as proficient as he was in the Ars. However, Turbatus seemed to have one, major fault. Perhaps it wasn't just one but many. He didn't inherently have the rugged, coarse nature a powerful medicus was supposed to have. Deep within Turbatus was a fatherly tenderness that made him uncomfortable in the Refectorium. Alumno could sense it when Turbatus was assisting him with his lessons. That tenderness, it seemed, caused him to have doubts. Why were they doing what they were doing? Who were they benefitting? Why weren't they helping the people with their powers? Were they simply learning these things to become powerful? Was that all to it? And the histories, they never did go in depth about the rebellion. Who exactly was this vassal Unus? Where did he come from? Why did he try to rise up against Lord Casus? Why didn't Lord Casus kill him? Where exactly was he now?

And then there were the dreams. Every medicus, the deeper they got into their study of the Ars, it was said, the more troubled they became. Many had gone mad. But the dreams, blasphemous dreams, they troubled Turbatus. Dreams of Lord Casus being humbled, being defeated. Paying homage to another. They troubled him deeply.

Turbatus never mentioned any of this to Alumno. But the more time they spent together and the more Alumno progressed in his skills, the easier it became for him to discern the person of Turbatus, feel his mind and thoughts. Sometimes, it was as if Turbatus was consciously communicating these things to him. Urging him, that as he learned, to seek the answers to those questions. To seek the truth. Obviously, with all Turbatus knew, he had a nagging suspicion that he didn't have the truth. He seemed to want the young Alumno to keep the truth as his focus, to not learn in a vacuum.

Turbatus disappeared one day, just vanished. Alumno went looking for him in his private quarters and saw another medicus moving into the rooms that were Turbatus'. In the Refectorium, one didn't ask many questions. So, as hard as it was, he had to let it go and try to forget his wise mentor and only friend. But he remembered him again, a long time after. That day he first met the Veneficus. When one of the child Veneficus offered him a human hand with a ring on it. The same ring that Turbatus used to wear.

Alumno watched the bodies bustling about the kitchen, baking, mixing, peeling etc. All this for a troublesome intruder. Well, that was how they referred to him before he entered the city. There had been word in the Refectorium of a crazed, rogue medicus in Nox who was tormenting people and causing confusion in different cities. They had been told to beware of him and that he might be coming to the City of Magus. However, it was expected that he wouldn't dare. Then, all of a sudden, a notice was sent out to him, apparently also to Invidere, to camp on the outskirts of the city. That was all they knew. Of course there had been more than the usual glitches in the scared realms, illness and incantations gone wary, but no one ever suspected that the "troublesome intruder" had power of that magnitude, really. But look, he had only been in the city less than half a day and had already crushed the legend of the most powerful incantation ever, first employed by Lord Casus himself, conjured by a powerful medicus with the assistance of the Veneficus, breached the impregnable walls of the Refectorium in the most fantastic way, received adoration from both the Veneficus and every medicus in the Refectorium ex Astrum, driven off some of the greatest generals of Lord Casus' force and was now resting in the best suite in the building. The suite exclusively used by Lord Casus the Majestic himself. Also, not to mention, Prince Leo was preparing to dine, from the looks of it, on the most sumptuous meal ever to be served up here in the Refectorium. Wow, what a day!

"Medicus?"

"Uh, yes. Ready?" Alumno asked the head chef medicus.

"Aye. Everything is in readiness. How will you be taking it?"

"I don't know," Alumno replied. "I really don't know. I have no idea how even I shall get there."

Uncaring, the head chef medicus walked away. His job was done. It meant nothing to him if someone else couldn't preform their job. It won't be his head on a platter.

Alumno looked at the twelve layers of trays on the cart. His body was still aching and he was exhausted. He wouldn't make it up to the Corona. He looked around the kitchen and found he was alone. The other cooks were all gone and the, moments ago, busy and noisy kitchen, now echoed dead silence.

"You will cause I send you."

That was what Prince Leo had said.

"You will cause I send you."

His skill in the Ars wasn't enough. Nothing that he knew would help him. Not now. If he didn't get up there, the prince might get mad and then the Veneficus would surely kill him. They didn't care if he was mentally depleted, in pain and couldn't make it to the Corona.

"You will cause I send you."

One thing might help. Perhaps the power was in those words? Maybe he could access the power of Prince Leo through his spoken words. His words came out of his body, the very body that contained all his power. Therefore his words had to be laced with his power! They were products of his mind.

Well, it was worth a try.

Alumno pulled the cart into the general hall. Standing by it and closing his eyes, he meditated on Prince Leo's words.

"You will cause I send you. You will cause I send you. You will cause I send you."

A strange beam of light, so strong, that it felt like paste showered down on Alumno. It gracefully picked up both he and the cart and glided them through the different levels of the Refectorium. What shocked Alumno the most was that, instead of draining him of his energy, this light seemed to replenish him his strength. Reviving every cell in his body. He had never felt anything like it. It was completely refreshing.

Before he knew it, he was in the Corona. Prince Leo, who was seated by the window and gazing down at the city, now turned around and looked at him.

"It's about time you figured it out."

Rising and motioning to a table, he addressed Alumno.

"Come. Let's see what we have here to eat. We're both hungry."

"You like the wine," Prince Leo asked, leaning back in his chair after the meal, while swirling the wine in his golden goblet.

"Sure! Definitely," Alumno replied enthusiastically. "The best I have ever tasted. Ever!"

"Nothing compared to what we have where I come from. The vineyards are set in soil that is absolutely perfect for growing grapes. Perfect soil, perfect climate and expert hands that have been in the wine making occupation from the beginning of time."

Alumno was wide eyed. He took another sip of the wine and sucked on its flavor. His nipples hardened. Better than this?

Alumno wanted to ask where exactly was he from? How far was it? If he was a prince, who was the king? Did he, Prince Leo, know of Lord Casus? What was he doing here in Nox? And many other questions but he had been sternly warned by the Veneficus.

"Do NOT speak to him! Only speak when spoken to! Know that he lies! Everything that he says is a lie! Pay his lies no head," Prince Leo mimicked the exact words of the Veneficus in their exact voices and then smiled at him.

Alumno, with chills running down his spine, sat his cup down and sat up in his chair. The hairs on the back of his neck stood up.

"They're going to kill me, aren't they," he asked Prince Leo.

"Of course. Why not? If you were in their position, wouldn't you? You know and have seen too much. You were out there in the streets. You are the only person who truly knows what happened out there. How your precious Veneficus couldn't get the job done. You are sitting here with me. And as you are, you are learning more and more of the truth without me having to spell it out."

Alumno blinked. Somehow, he always knew it would come down to this. He had worked hard. He had out performed everyone he knew. He had always done what was expected of him. He had disciplined himself to be the best. And all for what? To end like this?

He looked up at Prince Leo.

"I want to follow you."

"Follow me? Who said I was going anywhere? I might like it here," Prince Leo replied waving his hand over the food and wine spread out across the table.

"We've heard that you've gone to other cities. There is no reason for you to stop here. You're going to the Fortress of Vorago even, aren't you?"

"And you want to go to Vorago to see your precious Lord Casus the Majestic?"

"No. I want to be with you. Go where you go."

"Well, aren't you the loyal one," Prince Leo offered sarcastically.

"You just said they are going to kill me."

"So, because you realize that the Veneficus is going to kill you and I have no apparent reason to, you want to follow me? What makes you think I want someone like that following me around?"

"I...."

"You're just trying to save your life Alumno. Besides, you don't even know what I'm doing here."

Alumno slumped back in his chair. It was true. He was just trying to use Prince Leo for his own safety and protection. He hadn't even known him an entire day and he was selfishly trying to exploit him and his power. But wasn't that the life that he lived? That of manipulation and craft? What choice did he have? Supposedly, he had no escape. His end was near.

He poured himself a cup full of wine and swallowed hard.

Chapter Three

"Noooo!"

Alumno knew what was going on. He was being attacked! His heart was about to explode inside his chest. He saw the faces of the Veneficus swirling about his bed. A phantom spike was driven into his head. He tried to scream but no sound came out of his throat. His body was paralyzed. They were going to torture him to death. They were going to make him suffer. He could see the Veneficus speaking in a cryptic tongue. He could smell and was choking on their vile breath. He felt his skin tearing off of him, being rent apart like paper. He felt his bones crumbling inside of him.

Help. Someone. Please. Help.

No one would come to his rescue. He knew and now realized that he would never again see the bleak sun battle thick, dark clouds over the City of Magus. He would never again breathe the incense saturated air of the city nor walk down its streets surrounded by awe. For him, there would be no more phasing through the levels of the Refectorium, no more displays of his learning and skill in the Ars. This was how he was going to die. Squealing like a pig being skinned alive beneath the hateful smirk of the Veneficus who smiled at him while wringing the life out of his agonized and abused body. Alumno could see now that this had always been his fate. He closed his eyes in surrender as a tear slid down the side of his face.

"You will cause I send you."

An explosion racked the building! Light flooded the entire room and Alumno, somehow, released from a death grip, gasped for breath. He heard screams. The Veneficus? The echo of voices sounded like them. But screaming? He could feel the light penetrating his body, strengthening his bones, healing his flesh, restoring his mind.

There was another explosion!

Alumno realized that he was floating in the air and as if in slow motion. Time had been slowed down. He was watching as Prince Leo, in the middle section of the Refectorium, released raw, explosive force from his body, splitting the Refectorium into two equal halves, from top to bottom, even down to the blood soaked abode of the Veneficus. Prince Leo seemed to remain suspended in the middle section of the building. Next, from that middle section, another burst of power from his body broke the halves into two, as if sliced and forming a cross through the center of the building.

Then in a final and largest explosion, with Prince Leo at its core, the four parts began to burst apart into other pieces, which in turn, broke apart themselves. Light searing everything apart. The other medicus swirling around as Alumno was, attempted to shield their eyes form the blinding light but, at the same time, were mesmerized by the greatest spectacle any of them had ever seen.

The Veneficus were screaming from pain and agony that had to be nothing short of extremely excruciating. All nine were spinning in torment around Prince Leo, and not by choice. Alumno could see the prince's eyes. They were blazing with an intense heat, anger, rage. He had never before seen such power, that extent of furor. It seemed as if that passion was melting the Veneficus alive, disintegrating their frames, liquefying them.

A terrible sight to behold.

It was all over as suddenly as it had begun. The natural pace of time restored. Alumno felt himself lying on some rubble and struggled to raise his aching body out of the debris. Books, ashes, half melted precious metal and jewels that once beautified and adorned the great Refectorium ex Astrum now lay everywhere. There lingered a heavy scent of burning and a haze now hung over the entire city, naked, it seemed under the moonlit night sky. Alumno rubbed his eyes and stared in amazement at where the magnificent building that he had called home for so long once stood.

Through the haze, he also managed to sneak a peak at a dark, hooded figure walking casually away and out of the city. Slowly and with a nonchalance that would suggest nothing out of the ordinary had just transpired. Alumno wondered if he would ever again see such greatness as was the man, Prince Leo.

THE CITY OF VITIOSUS

Chapter One

Prince Leo's chariot roared into the great city and through it's gigantic streets. He sat back, looking about him as Villicus eagerly prodded the absolutely fine black stallions forward. Villicus was happy, thrilled, excited. For generations his family had anticipated the coming of the great Prince Leo of Lux to whom, they had always remained faithful. They had kept and watched over the entire estate with the knowledge that one day, their prince would return to their dark country to restore the Standard of Light over this land that had once been known as Hortulus. They had never wavered in their loyalty to King Unus but had remained steadfast even when their entire world seemed to forget times past, the former glory that had perpetually rained over the land. Of how there was peace and all the people were happy. Of the endless festivals and feasts. The abundance of every necessity but most importantly, how there was once honor in every heart. Now, it was all the stuff of legend, old wives tales. But he, Villicus, knew as his fathers had always known, that it was all true. There was a king, a rightful king and that his name was Unus. He was mighty and just. He was powerful and kind and that one day he and his noble son would return to claim what was theirs and restore perfect order. He had known! He had always known!

Villicus remembered the day his father passed into the hands of death. He too bore the name Villicus as had all his fathers. But the dear man was old, very old and scared. He had begun to wonder if the king had indeed forgotten that the people of Nox were rightfully his people. He wondered if the king would ever remember them, return to them and deliver them. The old man had waited eagerly his entire life, hoping and praying that he would one day behold the prince within the gates of the City of Vitiosus and in the great house. He had always told him when he was a boy how he would take the prince to the tomb of his fathers and show him were laid the men who were faithful to the magnificent City of Sedes, its king and its lord the prince. The tombs of the men who had always watched diligently over the estate in Vitiosus, the mansion, the printing press, the farms and charities. But as he grew old, his father began to despair. When was the prince coming? Was he ever coming? Everyone of his fathers had been certain that the prince would come in their own time and while they were alive. Had it not been too long already? But they all died without seeing their life's dream come true. Then his father too, as he held his father in his arms right before he passed away, cried. He had tried to exhort his father to believe, that the prince would come and that Lux had not forgotten its people suffering under

Casus' wicked rule. He remembered his father's last words.

"Now, you believe my son. You wait. I can't anymore."

And he did carry on the family belief. He did wait. He did carry on the family name of Villicus. And now, he drew the chariot of the prince, bearing him into the city! Oh, if only his father were here with him driving the horses! Of course he, himself, was now old. He had buried his father so very, very long ago and had no children of his own. He had begun to wonder how the family name would continue and if the prince didn't come in his lifetime, who then would carry on the task of maintaining everything. In his grandfather's and great grandfather's time, there were very few families who still bore in their hearts oath to King Unus. It was hard, even then to find a wife. In his own time, therefore, it had been downright impossible to find a believing woman in this wicked city. The women were all crazy and undisciplined. There would be no way he could find one who could in anyway resemble an honorable daughter of Lux and bear and help him raise a believing child to carry on the family work. His own mother had died when he was still very young and he had only known his father, his honorable and devoted father. And as his own years began to wade, his only terror was that he might die without leaving a son to walk in his footsteps and the footsteps of his fathers. Now, he had nothing to fear.

They drove through the busiest parts of the city, vividly awake in its morning bustle, and into a more quiet and secluded part of the city where the Mansion Umbra lay. Today, unlike most mornings, Villicus frowned on the throng that gathered at the gates, begging food. He shooed them away as he halted the horses and proceeded to open the gate.

"Come back later! When the master is resting and I'll have some food for you then!"

Villicus led the horses through the gates, and drove them up to the front of the mansion.

Prince Leo alighted the chariot and looked up at the relief over the door. It was of a man holding high a torch; it symbolized the holding high of the Standard of Light.

"Yes. Yes, my lord," Villicus said coming up to him. "My family has tried to do just that for many moons. For generations."

Prince Leo looked down and into the face of Villicus. He saw in his face, the faces of his fathers and his fathers' fathers. He saw their pain and dedication.

"Take me to them."

"My lord?"

"Take me to your fathers."

"I know you are tired and might want to rest. Maybe later? I have hot water ready for your bath and...."

"No, Villicus. That can wait. I must honor them."

A tear escaped the eyes of Villicus. He grabbed the arm of Prince Leo and led him to the back of the mansion, almost running. He felt it. It was almost as though, their dead spirits cried out to see their prince to whom they had been faithful and for countless moons. A family with a history of love and loyalty.

Villicus, weeping the whole time, hurriedly opened the gate to the tombs and led the way down.

Insurrectum Ex Lux Lucis

" Here my lord! Here," Villicus said rushing over to the biggest tomb and rubbing his hands against the stone. "The first Villicus after the insurrection of vile Casus. This one. He would not join Casus and his fiends when they wanted to take over the whole land of Hortulus. This one here, he stood firm. He was one of the governors, remember? You were around during that time. They tortured him. They beat him. But no. He stood firm," Villicus said pumping his fists, his face wet with tears, his pride in his heritage evident. "They did whatever they wanted to him but he and a few others refused to have anything to do with their nonsense! After they had turned everyone and set themselves up, they let them go. Villicus, this one, he came back to his home and found it burned down to the ground and everything in ruins. He started restoring it with no help from anyone. He knew you would come back to help the people. He knew it! And, he and his wife started fixing the place up so that you could come here, to this mansion you had given his family before all this nonsense. He didn't finish though. He was high up on a wall working one day when he fell to the ground and right before his young son, too. His son stood there and watched his father's body come crashing down to the ground before him. He," Villicus went over to the next tomb, "felt his father's blood and brains splatter against his face. And he swore to...."

But Prince Leo remained there over the first tomb, looking at the engraving of the face and running his fingers over the relief. Yes. He remembered Villicus, that first Villicus. How could he ever forget him? That first Villicus.

It was the dead of night in the City of Vitiosus and most of the city's denizens were deep in sleep. All was still and calm and dark as lamps had long been put out, being that there was no longer any need for light. Except, that is, in the Caputolium, the gigantic, black marble building in the heart of the city. It was the center of all important occasions, discussions, gatherings and its large open air halls were the site of many teachings and learning from all over Nox. It also held the city's famous library. Tonight, however, the central most hall was in use.

Imperator Decus, bearing the appearance of a handsome man, tall and of an impressive physique, glared at the other five Imperators assembled in the hall with him. Rage was clearly evident in his voice and tone.

"It is TOTALLY unacceptable that I should have to flee Magus before Prince Leo! Can you all appreciate the SHAME here?!"

"I have been saying the entire time that we should have killed him the moment he set foot on Nox," snarled Imperator Homicida, big and burly, priming with gigantic muscles.

"It isn't like we haven't been trying," said Imperator Avidas. Imperator Avidas was stout and round, with chunks of chubby, rosy cheeks. Most unsightly.

"We ought to have tried harder then! I simply cannot bear the fact that that pompous buffoon is here, on our soil. I personally loathe the very air he breathes," Imperator Odium retorted. Imperator Odium was tall and slender but with a solid build. His eyes were his most dominant feature, however. They always burned with the fires of unrelenting hate.

"What we ought to occupy ourselves with now, is a story, or stories, we should spread among the people to cover up this mess," Imperator Dulos chimed in. Imperator Dulos was lanky, with a long pale face. He seemed to be nothing but skin and bones.

"Being that the prince has destroyed the Refectorium," Imperator Pravus inquired, "where shall we consolidate and teach our craft?"

Imperator Pravus was simply disgusting to behold. He wasn't ugly, definitely not handsome. Primarily, he was just repulsive. His teeth were horrid, his breath torrid and his skin was even paler in appearance than Imperator Dulos. His finger nails were long and terribly unkept. The same with his hair.

"Lord Casus never should have ordered us to leave the Refectorium ex Astrum," said Imperator Decus. "We should have stayed and fought with the Veneficus. The loss of the Refectorium is the worst humiliation and I have severe doubts as to how we can recover."

"Stayed to have an end like the Veneficus?" Imperator Homicida asked sarcastically. "I think not. Lord Casus made the right decision. All this shows, however, that we must now focus on killing the prince as soon as possible. This toying must end now!"

"Who knows," Imperator Avidas added, "what new powers we might amass by killing the Prince of Lux, King Unus' own son."

"I think we must first reestablish our ways among the people. Make them continue to live and act as we want them to," pleaded Imperator Pravus.

"I agree," concurred Imperator Dulos. "We must reaffirm our hold over the people. We must give them our version of everything that is happening. Otherwise, we risk their thoughts beginning to wander. We can't allow them to think for themselves."

Imperator Decus, however, was still troubled.

"I am bothered by what has been happening so far. The situation, frankly, seems to be out of control. I'm thinking, the only chance we have of beating this, is for us all to combine our powers, act as one. What is Lord Casus saying about this?"

"His word is to wait," replied Imperator Dulos.

"His word got us into this entire mess in the first place! 'Overthrow King Unus!' he said. 'Take over Sedes and the entire land of Lux!' he said. We never should have followed him back then," roared Imperator Odium.

"The past is the past. We can't change what's happened and what we had part in. We must focus on the present and on maintaining control over what we have now," said Imperator Pravus.

"I don't know about the rest of you, but I don't want to step out and act and be further humiliated," Imperator Decus uttered. "Let us wait as Lord Casus suggests. Then we can all combine our powers with that of Casus and Imperator Metus who is always with him. That will be our best chance to defeat the prince."

The others thought about it.

"I still say we try to kill him and as soon as possible," said Imperator Homicida.

"He stinks of his father," added Imperator Odium.

"Well, no one is stopping you two from continuing to try till Lord Casus is ready," offered Imperator Decus. "I simply want no share in the embarrassment."

"But I want share in the credit if you should be successful," said Imperator Avidas. "I will offer help till then."

"In the meantime, I will find some tale that should appease inquiring and restless minds," Imperator Dulos declared.

"While I make sure the maggots continue to live and think like the filth that they are," added Imperator Pravus.

"You know," said Imperator Odium, "that that swine of a prince is already here, in the city."

It was as if a cold bucket of freezing water was poured over them. They remained as if frozen for a while. Finally, Imperator Dulos spoke in a low tone.

"Send Corruptela to see him."

Chapter Two

Late that morning, Prince Leo sat on the balcony in the back of the mansion overlooking the garden. It was beautiful. It reminded him of the many, many gardens back home, in Lux. The flowers seemed to display every color imaginable in a brilliant array and the shrubs were perfectly trimmed. To think, the family of Villicus had been tending this place for generations faithfully awaiting his visit but not knowing when exactly he would show up, if at all. Each of those generations, hoping, wishing, that he would come in their time. Each of them dealing with the disappointment of that dream never turning into a reality as age slowly surrendered them into the hands of their final life's end. The honor and legacy of this family could never be forgotten.

Prince Leo looked down at the books that lay sprawled open before him. He had been doing some reading. Perspectives of primary doubt from Dubito, the Picturae belief from the men of Artes to the north of Nox, hailings of the inevitable fate from Despero, the Numinis doctrines, beliefs of the citizens of Timidus north of Spes, the Solitus lifestyle and the list went on. Interesting concepts of life the people of Nox had developed into systematic thought. However, all of them were hollow and without a central, solid core. But sufficient ideologies to keep lesser minds in an almost perpetual swirl. And exactly what all these perspectives were intended to do. He, Leo, knew for a fact that all this was the genius of a certain Imperator Dulos. Confuse the people. Twist them, trip them up, occupy them, keep them under control, frustrated, disenchanted, disillusioned and in check. That was the name of the game that Casus was playing with Dulos' offering his services. It was, however, good and effective strategy.

Villicus came out unto the balcony.

"Sorry to bother you my lord, but you have a guest."

"Thank you Villicus. I'll see her out here."

"Yes my lord."

Villicus turned to leave but then hesitated.

"My lord, this woman is of the most notorious reputation. A ghastly creature. It would be my pleasure to send her away from here."

"I know Villicus. I know. Nevertheless, lead her out here."

"Yes my lord."

Prince Leo ran his fingers along the edges of the stack of paper piled up beside the open books. There was a small vile of ink with a golden feathered pen stuck in it. He wondered, what did it feel like to have the wool pulled over your eyes so that you couldn't see what was actually before you. But instead all you could see was someone's else's sick perversion of reality. How did that feel? How did it feel to be drowning under water, looking up at the surface just a few feet ahead of you but not being able to reach it because someone had their hand over your head, keeping you under?

"My lord Prince Leo. It has been a while," said a female voice behind him.

"Yes, Corruptela," Prince Leo answered without turning around, "it has been a while indeed."

"Have you missed me?" she asked approaching him from behind.

"I have missed all of you. This whole business is quite, shall I say, unfortunate?"

"I didn't ask about all of us, I asked about me. Did you miss me?" she persisted, now snaking her hand around the curve of his neck and down towards his chest.

Prince Leo grabbed her hand and pulled it toward the seat across from him before letting go.

"I see your time here has relieved you of your manners and you obviously have forgotten who I am," Prince Leo chided.

She sat across from him, rubbing her hand and staring at him.

"While you, on the other hand, haven't changed."

"Some things change, some people never change."

"You haven't answered my question. Did you miss me?"

"I did answer your question. You just didn't like the answer."

She sat there in silence, staring at him. Then she looked away and spoke softly into the air.

"I loved you."

"You loved my power, my status."

She looked back at him.

"I wanted you."

"You wanted power, glory. More glory than you already had."

"Why do you only hate me when I only love you?"

"I don't hate you Corruptela."

"Then why is it so difficult for you accept the way I feel about you. Why do you so want to believe that I don't love you? Aren't you lonely?"

"You have no idea what I am," Prince Leo responded. "How could you possibly love me in the way that you say?"

"I love whatever it is that you are."

"Really?"

"Really."

"Then why are you here and not back in Lux, if indeed, it wasn't power you were after?"

Her gaze drifted away.

"That's what I thought."

"You wouldn't understand," she responded almost in a whisper.

"Why not try me?"

She looked him in the eyes, her anger apparent.

"Prince Leo of Lux, Lord of Sedes and Son of King Unus, Master of All Lands, would you happen to have any idea whatsoever of how it feels to want to be something better than what you are? Have you any inkling of an idea?"

Prince Leo returned her gaze, but remained steady and calm. He allowed her words to hang in the air before he spoke.

"So, tell me Corruptela, are you better? Are you better here in Nox, than what you were in Lux? No, instead, answer me this, are you even a shadow of who you were before?"

Her eyes evaded him.

"We all regret the choice we made."

"Some regret. Look at what you all have been doing to these people," Prince Leo insisted.

"Well what would you have us do?! Just lay around waiting for whenever time you and your father should search us out and crush us? We made a mistake! That's all it was. A mistake."

Prince Leo raised his hand to his chin, massaging it while looking down at his papers.

"Terrorizing these innocent people," he said slowly, as if delicately picking the words out of the air, "...is another...BIG...mistake."

Villicus stood and watched her carriage roll away. He had so many questions, so many. Why hadn't the prince killed her, right here! That woman, or shell of a woman, was the most evil person he had ever had the misfortune of meeting. Some said that her age was a mystery. They said that she was very old. But her age didn't show. She was the most beautiful and enchanting woman in the entire land of Nox. He remembered his father had told him that their family believed that she had come to Vitiosus when the rebellion first started. That would make her generations old. But no man could hardly ever imagine it simply by looking at her. Most men would be turned into utter fools by just one wink from her, but somehow, that didn't work on him. He, Villicus, hated her! With a passion. His family hated her. His father and his father and his father's father hated her. And with rolls and rolls of passion.

That lady, going there, took little girls and young destitute women, and made them into harlots! Forced them to do things that they in their natural minds couldn't fathom. Beat them, tortured them, made them become evil like her, made them become slave catchers like her, harlots like her, sold them to men who were nothing more than beasts, who had no conscience and who treated women like animals! She sold them to the Men of Scelus who are wicked beyond any imagination. That woman there glamorized herself so much so, that the little girls of Vitiosus, admired and wanted to be like her. Like her! That abominable wench! Young women with virtue and promise, destroyed because of her. It was said that men who slept with her lost their Intimus Essentia, that scared thing that makes a man a man! They would lose this. Yet, there was no tally for the number of men who would gladly give and risk any and everything in order to be seduced by her. That accursed, villainous wench!

A hand touched his shoulder. Villicus spun around in his rage and saw the face of Prince Leo, looking into him.

"Let it go Villicus. It will only destroy you."

"My lord, that woman, she...she...."

"Villicus?"

Villicus tried to calm himself down.

"My lord?"

"Let it go," Prince Leo said, his voice trembling with compassion. "Casta made her decision and unfortunately, there is nothing either you or I can do about that."

"It was that woman my lord. It was that woman! She did it! It was her fault! Casta didn't know. I tried to tell her but she wouldn't listen. That wo...."

"Villicus?"

Villicus could hardly hear. He could hardly hear anything. His pain was so sharp, so deep and his heart wound still fresh. He was taken back to another time, a long, long time ago. When he was young, full of life, excited about life and, in love. A young girl close to his own age, but beautiful and gentle as the fresh, soft, silky petal of a rose. She was pure. She was his Casta. He loved her and she loved him. He could still remember how she smiled and blossomed into a blush every time she saw him. He could still remember how he would shiver inside every time she did that.

He could still taste the cakes she baked for him, the grapes she would feed him as they laid down to picnic on the luscious green grass after he had borne her on his back through the lonely fields on cool evenings. He could still hear the music her voice made when she spoke, could still see the every grace of her movement, the sparkling light in her eyes. He remembered she was soft. He would rest his head upon her lap and in no time dose into wondrous places. She was wonderful. She was everything any man could ever want. But....

...she admired the Lady Corruptela. She admired the way she carried herself with that defiant air. She admired the way men looked at her in drooling lust. She admired the way the Lady Corruptela could get anything she wanted. She admired her power and her influence over people, over the city. She admired how "free" and "unfettered" the Lady Corruptela was. He had out done himself trying to convince his lovely Casta that she really didn't want to be like Corruptela and that there was nothing to admire about her and her awful ways. He had tried to tell her that his family had believed that she was part of a rebellion against King Unus, Lord of All Lands and that the king would one day return to punish Corruptela and those like her. He had tried to dissuade her from her wrong infatuations, tried to show her the truth. But to her, he just had his head filled with silly stories. How could he believe any of that about the Lady Corruptela?

Then, one day, his Casta was suddenly gone, disappeared. He must have searched the entire city for her, but in his heart, he knew where she had gone. Still, he didn't want to believe it. He couldn't accept it. His Casta would never abandon him, no matter how much she admired the Lady Corruptela. She would never turn her back on what they had and would have. They were supposed to be married. Raise children loyal to the king and children who would carry on the tradition in case the prince didn't come in his own lifetime. He loved her and she loved him.

After a few days, his father sat him down and told him to give it up. To forget Casta and the life that could have been. He told him that this was the fate of their family and those who chose to remain loyal to the king. He told him that there was nothing that he could do anymore and that everything was out of his hands. But he didn't listen. How could he? How could his father ever tell him that? His father must never have felt for anyone the way he felt about Casta. If he ever did feel love the way he, Villicus felt it, he would understand that it wasn't a thing you could just fling aside. He couldn't simply forget her. He couldn't simply erase her memory from his mind.

A few days later, after that conversation, as he was making a trip out of the city on some business for his father, he saw a lifeless body lying outside the city's walls. It wasn't an unusual sight but, some evil hand drew him to the side of the road and over to the body, the tortured, broken, beaten, lifeless body. He knew before he saw, but when he saw the face, he fainted.

"Villicus?"

Tears were flowing down his face. He was looking into the face of Prince Leo, Prince Leo of Lux. The prince was calling him by name.

"Yes my lord?"

"You must let this pain go."

Chapter Three

Furcifer was hungry and his stomach was voraciously rebuking him for it. He had to do something, but what? He was too well known down in the busier parts of the city. He had stolen and swindled the people so much, that they instantly recognized him a mile off. Many of them were still chasing him and trying to do him some harm for what he had done to them some while back. Half of those people, he hardly remembered except for the fact that they were perpetually chasing and harassing him. Why couldn't people let things go? You got swindled, forget about it. It's part of life, it happens to everybody sooner or later. But no, they had to take it personal. So now, he was having a hard time in the city. Besides, his odor didn't help either. He couldn't understand these people's obsession with water and bathing and all the hassle that came with that. And every day! Some of them, more than once a day! Why? Especially when most of them didn't have a well in their homes and had to haul endless pails of water from the wells to their homes everyday. Why make unnecessary work for yourself? You could be doing something else like resting, relaxing in a shade or something. But no, they had to haul pails and pails of water all the way to their houses to bathe and to wash their houses even though both they and their houses were going to be dirty by the very next day. Then they'd have to do it all over again, and the next day, all over again, and the next day, all over again. Stupid! His tribe, the Nequam, had it right. They were a city unto themselves and never bothered to stay in any one place, washing and scrubbing or any of that nonsense. The only work they did was to swindle and steal to upkeep themselves for the day. Other than that, they just sat around and relaxed most of the time. What sense did it make to haul stones, make mortar, to build a house you're going to have to scrub and clean every single day? Why? These people build a house to take care of them, but are too dumb to realize that they spend most of their time taking care of it.

Well, whatever. But for now, his stomach was growling and he needed something to eat. He had heard that there was a mansion over in these parts of the city where they sometimes gave out food. He usually like to earn his food by stealing it or swindling someone or luring them into an alley and clubbing them over the head and taking their money. But he had become famous and that wasn't good for business.

That mansion there, with the crowd at the gate, that must be the one. He wondered how generous the folks were who lived there. It had been a while since he had quite a bit to eat. He approached the gate and began to stand there with everyone else.

"My, what's that smell?" someone asked.

"It's this filthy Nequam," another replied.

"Huh? A Nequam?" a burly man asked spinning around. Setting his eyes on Furcifer, he said, "I know you! You stole my money for my business!"

"Uh? It wasn't me," protested Furcifer, vaguely recognizing the man. "How can you be sure it was me?"

"I'll know that measly, little face of yours anywhere," the man said approaching Furcifer. "It's because of you that I'm here begging, you dog. I'm going to kill you!"

"What?! Over some money?"

The man swung at Furcifer, who dodged the blow.

"Don't let him get away," someone else cried. "He's known all over the city for that."

Just my luck, Furcifer thought, as he dodged another blow and the crowd encircled him. He was now looking for a way to escape and couldn't see one. Except, maybe....

He sprung at the gate, and with cat like agility, climbed it onto the other side. The crowd of people were screaming and jeering at him. As he jumped down, he looked up and stared at them in confusion. He couldn't for the life of him, understand why they were acting like this, like animals. They were going to kill somebody for swiping a little bit of money? What was happening to the world?

He casually walked up the driveway, ignoring the clamorous noise behind him. This was a nice place. One of the nicest ones he had ever seen. To think, someone lived here. That would be nice, but, after a while, wouldn't it get boring. The same place, the same location. Oh well, he didn't live here. Why should he care?

He thought about going up front, but then knew the door there would be bolted most likely. Plus, the kitchen wouldn't be at the front of the house now would it? And the main reason he was here was due to the urging of his stomach. So after inspecting the architectural designs at the front of the mansion, he proceeded towards the back

Upon reaching there, he discovered a vast expanse of garden, adorned with beautiful flowers. He hadn't before seen many gardens and so this one had him spellbound. Being of the Tribe of the Nequam, he was a lover of nature and the out doors. He wanted to see the entire garden, everything. There was a balcony on the back of the house and so he hastily climbed up on to it but almost fell off when he saw someone sitting at a table covered with books and paper, writing. The man didn't look up at him but he was certain he knew he was there. He had made a rustle of noise getting up there. Anybody else would have been asking who was over there and why were they climbing up. Nevertheless, he continued to climb over, onto the balcony, and tried to admire the garden but was distracted by the man, who knew he was there, but didn't look up at him nor speak to him.

"The garden is very nice."

The man ignored him and kept on writing.

"The garden is very nice," he repeated, a little louder than before.

But the man continued to ignore him. Furcifer found this to be somewhat disturbing. Then he thought that perhaps the man was deaf. So he walked over to the table and tapped on it.

"Hold on, I'll be with you in a moment," the man answered, again without looking up.

"Can you hear?" Furcifer asked.

"I could ask you the same question?" the man said again and without looking up. "I just told you that I'll be with you in a moment."

"Oh. Sorry."

Furcifer felt stupid. But what could be so important that this man didn't care when a complete stranger appeared on his balcony in the back of his house? He stood there looking around nervously, drumming the palms of his hand against his thigh.

"By all means, sit down," the man said, without as much as a glance in his direction.

Furcifer sat down and looked at the books. A lot of books.

"There," the man said, finally raising his head from what he had been writing. "Sorry if I appeared rude, I simply wanted to complete a thought."

"Oh no. No. Not at all. I am sorry for interrupting," Furcifer replied nervously. This man was strange, stranger than anyone he had ever met.

"It is an extraordinary view," the man said looking past him.

"What?"

"You were talking about the garden earlier."

"Oh? Oh yes. The garden. Yes. Extraordinary."

Furcifer paused, confused. Then he asked,

"Who are you?"

"I am Leo, Prince Leo."

"Prince? Prince of where?"

"We can talk about that later. For the moment, how about we get you something to eat?"

"Yes. Yes. I like you already. My kind of fellow. My kind of prince. Bring me something to eat," Furcifer said, leaning back in his chair.

Prince Leo got up and went inside the house. He soon returned.

"Villicus will be bringing something out in a little bit. For now, let me clear these books and things out of your way."

Prince Leo began clearing away the books and papers. Furcifer watched him in amazement. What was going on? Was this fellow for real? He was growing more and more suspicious by the minute. Was this some sort of setup? Perhaps this Leo fellow was actually calling in the crowd at the front gate to come take him away? But all his suspicions went away when he saw an older man approach with a tray of food and begin to set everything up before him. Still, he eyed everything suspiciously, watching the older man. Villicus? Did the prince fellow say Villicus?

Prince Leo apparently knew what he was thinking so he began to sample some of the biscuits and warm meal.

"Alright, alright. I gather it's not poisoned. Don't eat it all. I'm the one hungry here," Furcifer complained.

"Enjoy," Prince Leo said to Furcifer as he began to gorge himself.

Late that night in the shadows of the dark halls of the Caputolium, two figures clad in black spoke in low tones.

"So what did Corruptela gather from her meeting with our dear prince,"

Imperator Decus inquired of Imperator Dulos.

"Unfortunately, not much. But then, it is Prince Leo that we are talking about. We ought not to be surprised. She did say, however, that he had many books out on a table before him."

"Books? What books?"

"My books. The ideas and lies I'm feeding the people. You know, the ususal nonsense, primary doubt, inevitable fate, the Numinis trash and the rest."

"Why would Prince Leo be reading those?" asked Imperator Decus with obvious concern.

"I don't know. I'm not sure. It's a mystery to me."

Silence issued.

"Is that all he had on the table?" Imperator Decus asked. "Did Corruptela say whether or not he had something else on the table? What else was he doing? Anything."

"She happened to mention that he had some paper and ink. I think that's what she said," answered Imperator Dulos. "A lot of paper and some ink. Writing and studying or something of the sort. Quite strange isn't it?"

Imperator Decus stood there pondering for a while. He paced a few steps and then suddenly cursed in an arcane tongue. He punched at a pillar and cracked it, spewing dust about them as pieces of the stone pillar crumbled to the ground.

"What?" asked Imperator Dulos. "What is it?!"

"Curse you fool! Can't you see? He's writing a book!"

"A book?"

"Yes! A book! A book that will show the entire land of Nox how stupid your lies really are! We've got to do something."

Imperator Dulos stood there in complete and utter shock. How could this be happening? But of course, it made sense! They all knew that Sedes was briefed on everything they did, the lies they told the people, the way they forced them to live, everything. So it wasn't like Prince Leo didn't know what the people believed and what they were reading. The only reason why he would now be studying the books was to systematically quote and refute them in a book of his own. One by one, every foolish ideology of Nox would be stripped bare and naked and exposed for what they truly were, a pathetic string of senseless fiction.

"What do we do?" he asked Imperator Decus. "We have to try to stop him."

"Imperator Odium was right," hissed Imperator Decus. "We never should have followed that wrenched Casus. I ought to still be ruling under King Unus, not going through one embarrassment after another."

"You have to help me," Imperator Dulos pleaded. "We have to do something."

"Where in the city is the prince," Imperator Decus demanded.

"He's at the Mansion Umbra."

"The Mansion Umbra?"

"Yes. It's the mansion built by the Villicus family, the one that still remains loyal to King Unus."

"The Villicus family? You mean, they're still around? Wasn't Corruptela supposed to insure that they died out? No wives, means no children! No children, means the family tradition dies!"

"Calm down Decus. She did kill off the future bride of the last Villicus but he is still alive and he's old. He has no son and so the family tradition dies with him."

"Well, it's a little too late now. Prince Leo is here."

Imperator Decus thought for a while.

"Mansion you say?"

"Yes. The mansion is in one of the secluded corners of the city," Imperator Dulos responded.

"How is the Villicus family up keeping a mansion?"

"The family has maintained some of its properties from before the rebellion. They own farms, vineyards, a few charities, but mainly a...."

Imperator Dulos froze and he felt his heart stop.

"And what?!" Imperator Decus demanded.

"A printing press," Imperator Dulos whispered. "The largest in Vitiosus."

Furcifer lay on the grass in the garden, looking up into the night sky. It felt good, a full stomach did. He had completely forgotten what one felt like. Still, he kind of felt bad that he didn't earn his meal. Oh well. One had to take charity from time to time. He was nevertheless, glad that there was still some human goodness left in the world. They had even offered him a room in the mansion, but he had declined. He preferred the cool night's grass for his bed and the canopy of the sky over his head. Those men were really nice. The nicest he had ever met. The younger one was really strange though. No matter, he would just snatch a few moments sleep and wake up later, when it was still in the dead of night, slip into the house, and steal a bunch of valuables. Since they had been kind to him, he won't bash them over the head to make sure they were unconscious while he went through the house. He'll simply be extra careful not to wake them. They were nice fellows.

As he lay there, enjoying himself and surrounded by the scent of magnificent flowers under the moist night sky, under a blanket of descending fog, he began to dose off. Then he heard a sound. He glanced about him but didn't see anything, so he didn't think nothing of it and tried to get to sleep. But out of the corner of his eye, he saw dark figures in a cross-legged, sitting position, floating in the air above the garden headed towards the house. This scared the wind out of him and he felt a lump in his throat. He got up softly, so as not to make a rustle of a sound and draw attention to himself. He whisked himself over to a shrub and hid in it.

Medicum. Those were medicum from the City of Magus where they practiced the Ars, secret, mystical arts. He had heard about them, knew where their city was, and had vowed never to go anywhere near there. All that stuff was frightening to him. He didn't understand it and neither did he ever want to. Those things were unnatural. But now, nine of them were headed for the mansion. He wanted to get away but was afraid to risk being noticed. He was terrified.

Imperator Homicida planted his feet amongst the shrubs of the garden. So did Imperators Odium and Avidas. They were here to support the nine medicus assassins with power from their very own Intimus Essentia, their essence. But the truth was, they were scared. They didn't want Prince Leo to see them. Of course the nine attacking medicus didn't know this. They foolishly believed what they were told. That there was no reason for the Imperators to kill this fellow themselves. But they, the nine medicum, were to be honored that they were chosen to preform this special task. They were to fear nothing. Weren't three of the Imperators going to be right there with them, supporting them with their own strength and power?

But at least the three of them were brave enough to try, Imperator Homicida thought to himself. Imperator Decus was too scared to make an attempt. "I don't want to be embarrassed. I don't want to be ashamed." Crying like a frightened, little girl. But, at least he had these two with him. They weren't afraid. They weren't trying to hide behind the group. At least they had it in them to act. If things didn't go well, the three of them could safely escape. Hopefully.

He closed his eyes as he started to meditate.

Leo, wake up.

It was the voice of his father, King Unus. Prince Leo opened his eyes and turning his head on his pillow, saw that his bed was surrounded by dark figures with swords and axes drawn. He sprang up, tossing his bed sheets over half of them. Then he spun around and kicked the one closest to his head. The movement was so quick, the assassin hadn't time to react. The impact of the kick sent him sprawling into two others. Prince Leo decided to take this outside.

He jumped through the window and out onto the backyard before the garden. Two immediately followed him, swinging their swords. Prince Leo landed on the ground below and instantly jumped back into the air toward one of them, knocking him unconscious before he even touched the ground. Prince Leo landed back on the ground, picked up his sword, blocked the attack of the other and slashed him across the stomach in one swift motion.

Now it began to rain medicum, as the remaining seven descended, certain that they were going to kill their prey. The three Imperators in the garden knew better and vanished in billows of black smoke. One medicus ran up to Prince Leo with his sword drawn high. Prince Leo blocked the strike and stepped forward with his sword, slitting his opponent's throat. Another attacked Prince Leo from behind with an upward swing of his sword from his right side. Prince Leo blocked that swing with a powerful counter swing, almost knocking the weapon out of his opponent's hand, and then brought his sword up to block another attack, in the upward process, slashing his opponent across the mid-section. Half facing the assassin whose downward axe strike he had just blocked, he kicked him in the mid-section and chopped his left arm off at the shoulder. Another axe came at Leo horizontally and from behind. Prince Leo stepped back out of its way, kicking further back the now one-armed medicus behind him. He threw his sword at the chest of the axe swinging medicus where it settled perfectly. The remaining two became enlightened and ran away.

By then, Villicus had heard the noise and came running outside to see what was happening. He hurried outside with a lantern in hand only to find the prince standing in the midst of two dead men, one slit in the throat and the other with a sword impaled in his chest, one man lying unconscious, two men bleeding from their mid-sections, and one freshly handicapped man, crying over his left arm lying before him in the grass.

Chapter Four

Furcifer awoke late that morning with a start. The sun was up and shining as bright as it could behind the thick clouds that always hovered over the land of Nox. He had planned to leave his hiding place amongst the flowery shrubs of the garden, earlier in the morning when it was still dark. He had been petrified by the things that he had seen the night before. The nine medicum floating in the air above him, the three strange men who entered the garden after them, stood not far from where he was, watched the issuing battle, disappeared in the middle of it and the bloody swiftness with which "the prince" disposed of, not one or two medicum, but nine. Well, of course two of them ran away. But who in their right mind could blame them?! Look at how that man moved against them! He had never seen anything like it. Ever!

He moved with purpose and with an uncanny fluidity. As if he expected everything to turn out exactly like it did. He didn't hesitate neither did he seem to over think what he was going to do. Again, he didn't hesitate. At all! To kill! How could a man who had been so kind to him the day before, not hesitate to take life? He couldn't understand that. There was a air of certainty about him, confidence, composure, self-control.... Yes, self-control! Last night, when he was dealing with those assassins, he didn't seem to move or attack them out of rage. It was like he was just moving, just walking or breathing. He was acting as if he was perfectly okay and comfortable with what he was doing. He wasn't scared or nervous. Nine medicum were swinging swords and axes at his head and he wasn't the least bit afraid!

What craziness was this?

Furcifer got up and looked around. No one was outside from what he could tell. It was time for him to get out of here as fast as he could. He didn't know what was going on or who that prince was but he wasn't sure that he wanted to find out. That man was dangerous. He alone handled nine medicum. Nine! It took only one to put he, Furcifer, into a terrible fright. That man alone dealt with nine. Plus, who were those three who watched everything from the shadows of the garden? They were even more eerie than the medicum. Yes, it was time for him to get away from this place. It was accursed.

Looking every which way about him, he crept out of the garden. Staying in whatever shadows he could find, he stealthily made his way away from the mansion and its grounds.

Insurrectum Ex Lux Lucis

Corruptela looked over the new girls brought before her. She half looked at them and half didn't. Truth was, she didn't want to see them. She waved at one of her head ladies to take them away from her sight. Within the minute, they were all gone and she was alone.

Sitting in a large golden chair in a lavishly decorated hall, she stared at her own reflection in the polished marble floor before her. When the Imperators asked her to go see Prince Leo, she was inwardly excited. She knew she shouldn't have been, but she was. She knew that they were now on opposing sides, but still, in her heart, Prince Leo was still Prince Leo, her prince. A flood of memories had flooded her mind. She remembered seeing him in Sedes, his city, the Crystal City. The prince had always been nothing short of magnificent. She adored him. Everything from the way he walked, turned around, talked, looked at you, looked in your direction, the way he looked at you when he spoke to you, everything about him was captivating. She had always wanted to be close to him, near him. To have him touch her. Maybe caress her. But it never happened.

He never did call her over privately, out from the crowd nor allow his eyes to linger on her. He never paid her any extra attention. Couldn't he tell that she loved him? He was wise, you could tell that he knew everything that went on around him. He was that kind of person. And all she wanted to do was to be near him. Walk with him when he spoke to the lords, nobles and governors. Be by his side when they came to give him reports of other lands. Was that so wrong? In essence, she wanted to be his wife. Imagine! The wife of Prince Leo, Lord of Sedes, Son of King Unus! That would make her Princess Corruptela!

But it was only a dream. Now that she thought about it, perhaps a dream that was not unique to her alone. She probably shared that dream with millions of other women in Lux. Hmm. She had never thought about it like that before. And that thought sent her into new depths of depression. Now, clearly she could see that she wasn't the only woman to think the things she did, but here she was and there those other women stayed. Safe and still wonderful in the land of Lux, close to Sedes and closer than she will ever be to Prince Leo.

She hadn't been just any woman in the realm. She had been one of the head Magistrae of the land of Lux, mother of women. She had a place of trust, power, prestige, influence. Women looked up to her to lead them and guide them in their way and the manner of feminine things. They came to her, the Lady, and they respected her. They loved her and adored her. What did those same women think of her now?

Back then, her role had been to nurture and develop persons of honor and dignity. To give young women instructions into womanhood. A woman who was a paradigm of virtue and of high esteem is not a thing of chance. It is an overwhelming task, role, to be a true woman in the purest form. It is a discipline, an astute discipline. A discipline to become a kind of woman that would make a man regard you with the profoundest esteem and admiration, desire with all his heart that a woman of your caliber would choose to stand by him and mother his children. Because, and that's a big because, he knows that no one else can do it like you can. Because he knows that you are able, that you would know what to do. You would be the wellspring of the home, a fount from which all members could come to drink when famished and lost of strength.

But now, and she smiled to herself a smile of self-pity and disgust, she taught the exact opposite. She didn't teach honor, dignity or self-respect. She taught young women how to exploit and be exploited at any means necessary. It was her responsibility to instruct and train young women how to carry themselves in such a way as to be lusted over, to digress from being women to becoming mere play things for gratification, to be seduced and ravished at random. Not to make men regard them with esteem and admiration or desire women to stand by them in a home, but to lay in submission in a bed. Not as a mother of his children to rear them up in that special way only a mother could, but only to be handy when he felt the urge.

She remembered the question. The question Prince Leo asked her. It kept playing and replaying itself in her mind.

"So tell me, are you better Corruptela? Are you better here in Nox than what you were in Lux? No, instead, answer me this, are you even a shadow of who you were before?

"So tell me, are you better Corruptela? Are you better here in Nox than what you were in Lux? No, instead, answer me this, are you even a shadow of who you were before?

"So tell me, are you better Corruptela? Are you better here in Nox than what you were in Lux? No, instead...."

Villicus drove the horses hard. He couldn't believe it! How would the prince react. After what he saw last night, he saw the prince in a whole new light. It wasn't that he was surprised, it was just that he was shocked. From generation to generation in his family, every father had told his son that King Unus and his son, Leo, were stern and their vengeance terrible. So out of habit, every generation had believed it. But at the same time, disbelieved it. If they were indeed as stern as they were supposed to be, why did they put up with what Casus was doing and put up with it for as long as they were? He had wrought open rebellion and took it to them in the heart of Lux, the magnificent City of Sedes itself. He had dared to stand up to both Prince Leo and his father, and to their faces! After that, he overtook one of their lands, did whatever he pleased and ruled it right under their noses for generations. How stern can one be and still put up with all of that?

But last night, Prince Leo killed with no emotion. By the time he arrived downstairs to find out what exactly it was that was going on, the prince had beaten nine medicus, killed two and fatally wounded five. As he shone the light of his lantern on the scene, Prince Leo walked calmly past him and, he later discovered, went soundly back to bed! Needless to say, he had a new found fear, if not dread, for Prince Leo, Son of King Unus.

He reigned in the horses at the front of the mansion and ran panting through its doors. He knew the prince was on the balcony at the back of the mansion, writing as he had been most of the time, and so headed straight in that direction.

"My lord! My Lord Prince Leo! It's bad! It's very bad!" Villicus went screaming even before seeing the prince.

When he finally got to the balcony, he met the Prince Leo sitting calmly at the table with his books, sipping grape juice mixed with water while looking out over the garden.

"Calm down Villicus. What is it?" the prince inquired.

"My lord, it's the printing press," Villicus said, trying to regain his breath. "It's been burnt! Burnt down to the ground!"

Chapter Five

Prince Leo walked through the garden in the back of the mansion. He walked slowly, careful to touch and caress the flowers. He took time to admire too, the stems, the leaves and the roots that made the beautiful, colorful flowers possible.

First, pain attacks us. Comes to us all of a sudden and tears at our soul so hard it leaves a mark. We cry out in shock and dismay as agony sets in. Then we realize, that more often than not, only more pain can rectify the wrong. More pain to heal the wound and return everything as it should be.

His feet led him to the tombs. The gate creaked as he opened it. The air inside was cool and damp and smelt of the gigantic stone it was chiseled out of. It was as if Prince Leo could feel the souls of the men, the dead men who built this place, Mansion Umbra. Expecting his visit. But expecting more.

He descended the stone steps, slowly, seeing his breath in front of him. It was as though, with each step, he met and passed one of the dead Villicus, starting with the most recent one who had died. Each of them telling him their own story. Telling him of how they had suffered, agonized, worried over and craved his coming. He finally got to the last step, met the first Villicus, and looked into his eyes.

"Redeem our land. Restore honor to our people. Resurrect us."

This was what their wait was about. The first Villicus hadn't simply rebuilt his mansion so that Prince Leo could come visit him as promised. This place was rebuilt as a demand to Sedes that the land of Nox not be forgotten or abandoned. The first Villicus defied the insurrectionist to their faces and upon brick and stone burnt by fire, vowed that his land would be returned to him and his family, his people. He built this place and made his sons and his sons' sons swear that this place would remain as a way of forcing the hand of Sedes, the hand of Prince Leo and King Unus. In effect, he was saying, "I won't lose hope neither will I give up. You MUST come and restore this land where my body lies and shine your light over my bones." That was what the engraving at the front of the mansion was saying. The first Villicus knew that he was going to die, so he engraved himself in stone, holding up a torch. Perhaps what would be the only light in a dark land. While his life and body would in time fade, the stone engraving facing the land of Lux would not. He remained there, in front of the Mansion Umbra, in Vitiosus, in the center of the land of Nox, holding up a light and saying to Sedes, "Look at me. Remember me. I am still here and I am still upholding the light."

"My lord? My lord, are you down there?"

Prince Leo could hear Villicus calling him and coming down the steps.

When Villicus arrived, he met Prince Leo leaning over the tomb of the first Villicus. Looking down into the engraving of the face as though he were looking at the face of a sleeping man.

"My lord?"

"Villicus?"

"Yes my lord?"

"Are you ready to sleep?"

Villicus' heart stopped. He knew instantly what the prince was asking. He was asking if he was ready to sleep as his father's slept here. He thought back over his life, his lonely life. He realized that he had never wanted much. He had never wanted to fail his fathers, that was for sure. He had dreamed of one day seeing the land of Lux. He had never truly been sure that Prince Leo would come in his lifetime, but he had always believed he would. He supposed, of all his fathers, he had had it best in the end. He actually did meet the prince. Drove him into the city. Though he had never known the love of a wife or a child, he knew that in the end he had had it best.

"Yes my lord. I am ready to sleep."

Prince Leo looked up at him with tears in his eyes, went up to him and embraced him.

"Thank you," Prince Leo said to him.

Villicus cried on Prince Leo's shoulder. Yes. Yes! He had it best. His life was worth something. He had carried the torch. He had been true to the oath he had sworn to the king on his knees with his father when he was only a little boy of four. He had been true to the oath his father had sworn and his father. All the way back to the first Villicus. All the way back to before the insurrection. The prince was not only thanking him, but his fathers and their fathers. He was thanking the first Villicus.

Prince Leo released Villicus, who was somewhat ashamed and was trying to wipe the tears off his face.

"Go lie down by your father," Prince Leo said to him.

Villicus went and laid himself down on the floor by the tomb of his dead father. He had always wanted to be amongst his fathers in this tomb when his time came. He had long given up on that dream since he didn't have a son. Without a son, who would chisel out a tomb for him? Every son had done it for his own father. He had thought of doing his own, but then, who would care to lay him in it?

But...he had it best in the end.

He lay there and closed his eyes and prepared to take his last breath. He was a happy, happy man. He didn't have a wife, he didn't have a son, but he wasn't and hadn't been alone. He had had his hope and in the end, he saw it manifested before him. His prince.

Villicus breathed his last and final breath.

Prince Leo raised his right hand out over the body. The stone floor began to rise up under and around the body of Villicus, forming a tomb very much like that of his fathers and engraving his face on its surface. Within seconds, the tomb of the family of Villicus was complete. Prince Leo turned away and left them to themselves.

Chapter Six

Mercator couldn't explain it. Of all his many, many years of trading and carrying merchandise all over the land, supplying Vitiosus with books from the many different cities, he had never encountered anything like this before. In his stocks and trains, were thousands upon thousands of these books entitled, Inconcessus Sententa. There was no author listed on them and he could swear that he had never before seen it. He always inspected copies of the books that he bought to sell to other cities, and even read a little bit of them and sometimes, actually met with the authors. But this, what was the explanation?

What was even more baffling, was the fact that people were buying these books as if they were possessed! The whole thing was making him a fortune. But who was the author? Didn't he or she want a percentage of the earnings. How did these copies end up in his storehouses and on his wagon trains? He usually didn't question his profits and often, well, always, he hiked up the prices of books he sold way above and beyond their value. But this...this was quite worrisome.

He sat in his mansion, his heart pounding in his chest. He had no idea what was going on around him and for once, he really cared being that it effected his business. But then, another thing he had to be concerned about was the fast depleting quantity of the copies that he had. At the rate at which people were buying the books, it was highly possible that he could be completely out in a matter of days. How would he get more copies? Especially since he didn't know how he had acquired the copies that he did have, didn't know the author or the city from which he got them.

He had no choice. There was only one thing he could do. He couldn't have people hounding him for a copy of a book that he didn't have in stock and didn't know how to get back in stock. He picked up his bell and rang for his aide. The man came running in no time.

"You know that strange book that we happened to have," he asked the man.

"Oh yes master. The people are buying copies of it faster than anything we've ever sold."

"Hmmm. And we still don't know who the author is, do we?"

"No. No one has come forward."

"Then we have no choice. Take a few copies and rush over to our own printing presses. Even take some to Dubito and start making as many copies as possible. We must never run out."

THE TRIBE OF NEQUAM

Chapter One

Furcifer left the City of Vitiosus and had decided to return to the Nequam, his tribe, his people. He had gone out and lived in the big city among the radix, the derogatory name his people had for those who lived out their entire lives in houses and in the same locale. He had experienced somewhat of their way of life and was more than certain that it wasn't for him. The idea even, was preposterous. It was like living like a tree. A tree, understandably, couldn't go anywhere. That was because it had roots in the ground that didn't permit mobility, moving around. But people on the other hand, they didn't have roots and that was for a reason. His people believed that people were meant to appreciate the land, all of the land. People were supposed to move about, from one place to another. Enjoy the way the breeze moved over the land, in the plains, in the mountains, in the valleys and through the forests. Pause by the side of the river, lie in the doorway of the caves as the rain lulled one to sleep. Now that was living. That was enjoying life and the land that one lived life on. The thing was, and the radix obviously couldn't understand this very simple fact, people aren't plants that you plant in one place and expect them to stay there till they died. People were more like animals, which were a higher and more intelligent form of life.

Besides, Furcifer thought to himself, some pretty strange stuff started happening in that there city and he wanted no part of it. That whole medicus thing, where they do strange things, abnormal things. Like those nine he saw hovering above his head that night. Really! What was that all about? Why do that? Why do something strange? Was there something wrong with their feet that they had to hover about? The radix always thought in opposites and he couldn't understand why. They labored building houses when the shade of a tree is cooler and perfectly natural. Caves. Nature's shelter from the elements. No. They have to build houses. Then they have to build houses close by each other. Then they have to build streets. Then they have to build buildings for those who have built their homes close by each other, to gather under one roof on special occasions. Then they have to build a wall around this place they call their city. And what next? Their whole thinking was in a tangled mess. But, he had to admit, the whole medicus thing was the worst.

Furcifer spun around. He could have sworn that he heard a twig snap. But there was no one there. Just the open country with a few trees sprinkled here and there. And this wasn't the first time it had happened. Ever since he left the city's walls, he could swear that someone was following him. But every time he turned around, he couldn't see anyone. What was going on? Was he losing his mind? Perhaps he had been among the radix too long. They were strange and when one was around them, strange things happened. Like that medicus nonsense.

What if, though, one of those medicus was following him? What if they had done one of their bizarre acts and was causing him not to see them, whoever it was? He really did feel as though someone was following him. But why would someone follow him? The radix didn't like the Nequam. They looked down on them. As hard as that was to imagine, it was true. So why would one of them follow him? But then, there was no end to the mystery of why the radix did some of the things that they did.

"Who's there? Come out!" Furcifer shouted.

His voice went out into the wind and over the land. There was no response. He looked around and as far as his eyes could see, he was the only sign of life. His heart was racing. He was scared. He felt as though something, someone was out there. He had felt that way since leaving the city. Most likely one of those abominable medicus. This was how they did things. Everything with them had to be bizarre, weird. Probably one of those that prince guy didn't kill. But why him? Why follow him?

All of a sudden, he wished he weren't alone. He wished he was among his people. They might not have had a city of stone, but they were a city unto themselves. They knew how to manipulate the colors of the open field or the dark forests. They could stand right in front of you and you wouldn't even know it. And there was some sort of safety in their numbers. Though they always ran away from a fight and many of the radix, especially the Men of Scelus, used them as game for their hunting exhibitions, they had always felt secure together and it didn't really matter whether or not that security was false.

"Fear Furcifer," a somewhat familiar voice said from behind a tree. "You have too much fear in you."

He knew it! Someone was out there. Someone had been following him. He started to run without even thinking about it. His feet automatically started running in the other direction, even before he recognized that it was that prince fellow, the strange, vicious one.

"Stay away from me," he yelled over his shoulder as he tried to get behind a tree that he saw ahead of him. But his feet stumbled over some branch or stone. Whatever it was set him off balance and he began to fall. As he landed on the ground, his head crashed into the trunk of the tree that he thought was a further away. Everything went dark.

His head! His head was killing him. The pain was unbearable. The throbbing. He managed to open his eyes and squinted at the flare of the fire crackling before him. He leaned his head back and rested it on the cool grass.

What happened? How did he end up this way? Oh, yes! That prince fellow. He raised his head up, a little too fast, and yelped in agony.

"Take it easy. You hit your head pretty hard against that tree," a voice said from across the fire.

"What are you doing here," Furcifer asked. "Why are you following me?"

"Actually, I'm not following you. It's just that we're going to the same place."

The same place?

"The same place? I'm going back to my people, the Nequam. I don't know where you're going."

"As I said, we're going to the same place."

"What do you want with the Nequam," Furcifer shot out. "You're a radix. Stay in one place your entire life. What happened to your mansion? The big house in the big city? Go back to it! Don't follow me."

"As we speak, Furcifer, the mansion is on fire. So like you, I have no house to live in."

"On fire? Why? What happened? Wait! How did you know my name?"

"Have you ever heard of Lux?"

"The fabled land of Lux? Yes, I've heard of it."

"I am Prince of Lux."

Prince of Lux? Was this fellow.... Wait. He had said that his name was Leo. The Prince of Lux's name was supposed to be Leo. According to the stories that is. This was nonsense.

"Lux is a fable. It's not real. It's just a made up story. No such place actually exists. If it did, the Nequam would have found it. We've traveled all over Nox...."

"Have you ever been past the Seven Mountains and the Seven Seas east of Nox?"

Furcifer fell silent for a while. Going that way was unheard of.

"Why would we travel there? There is nothing there but seas and mountains. Oh, let me guess. That's where the land of Lux is?" sarcasm lacing his voice.

"Look at the fire Furcifer."

Furcifer looked at the fire. It was fine. Nothing unusual about it. But then he began to see something in the flames. He began to see a place, bathed in light. There were tall buildings and little ones, all splendid. Cities, towns, villages. All looked very natural. The blend. The way things were. And then he heard voices. It was the voices of children, laughing and playing in the fields. Running about as they ought to naturally do. There were people sitting in the shades of trees gently swaying in the wind, sipping wine, talking, joking, laughing. Enjoying life, happy to be alive.

It was gone. All he could see were flames.

"What was that? Another trick? Where is this place?"

Prince Leo didn't answer him.

"Is it a real place? Is it? Is it Lux?"

Still no answer.

"Take me to this place. This place you just showed me. Take me there."

Again, no response. Furcifer couldn't see him on the other side of the fire. He could see an outline of him, but he couldn't really see him, his face. He didn't know what to think.

"Why are you going to the Nequam," Furcifer asked.

"To show them what I just showed you."

"Are you going to take them there then?"

"No."

"No? Why not? Why show them, why show me, if you're not going to take us there?"

"Because...I have something better in mind."

"What?"

"I'm going to bring that place to you."

Chapter Two

Prince Leo awoke with a start. His heart was racing and it was still in the dead of night.

Amidst the dark, marble halls of the Caputolium, Imperator Decus approached Imperator Homicida.

"So how did your attempt go?" he said with a smirk. "Did you manage to kill our unwelcomed guest?"

"Don't dare insult me!" Imperator Homicida roared. "At least I did something but sit here and cower!"

Imperator Decus' eyes flared to a burning red with anger. But slowly, he began to calm himself.

"No doubt, you've heard of my success. Had it not been for me, our dear prince would be a famous author. The most famous, perhaps, in Nox."

"Then you haven't heard. The prince may not be a famous author, but his book is all over the city and soon to be all over Nox."

"What!? Impossible! We burned the printing press owned by the Villicus family!"

"Well, like one of you said before, it is Prince Leo we are dealing with," replied Imperator Homicida, smug.

Imperator Decus was furious. Embarrassed. Again. Humiliated. Again. Made to look like a fool. Again. Proven inefficient. Again. How could things have gotten so out of control. How could they let one measly book slip through their fingers. And soon to be all over Nox?

"So, Imperator," Imperator Homicida said, obviously enjoying his fellow's bewilderment and frustration. "If you don't have anything positive to add to the situation, I suggest you go lick your own wounds instead of poking at mine."

Imperator Decus glared at him.

"Oh I've got something positive to add to the situation."

Beads of sweat were poring off of Prince Leo's body. The images he had just seen in his dreams. The horror of them.

"Furcifer! Furcifer! Get up! Now!"

"Ask yourself, Imperator Homicida. Why are we here," Imperator Decus' voice trembling with rage.

"What do you mean?"

"Why are we here? King Unus kicks us out of Sedes, out of Lux and so we are here. Why?"

"Quit the riddles and say what you have to say!"

"We are here to hurt King Unus and his whoreson, Leo. That's why we are here. To prick them were it hurts. These wretches they care about so much! So, for a change, let's jump ahead of our dear prince. We know he's headed for the Nequam...."

"....so kill the Nequam!" Imperator Homicida said finishing the sentence.

"The whole miserable lot of them. Maybe that will teach the Son of Unus to behave himself and give us some respect. Get your Men of Scelus out tonight. Find the Nequam and kill them all!"

"What? What do you want? Oh! My head! My head hurts," moaned Furcifer as he snuggled back to sleep.

"Get up! Your people, where are they?" Prince Leo pleaded. "You must tell me where they are."

"Why? Why should I? My head hurts. Stop shouting."

"Men from Scelus are looking for them to kill them. Get up. We must find your people."

"Men from Scelus? Is that what this is all about? Men from Scelus are always hunting my people. It's been that way since the beginning. There is nothing to worry about."

Furcifer dismissed Prince Leo and went back to sleep.

"Get up! Furcifer, this is not like before."

Frederick De Leon

"Leave me alone. Oh, oh! My head hurts. Go away. If you want to scream. Go far over there. Leave me alone."

Chapter Three

Furcifer looked around the forest valley smoldering in ash, wisps of smoke still swirling about from the night before. Broken and charred bodies lay everywhere. Men, women and children. The carnage was indiscriminate. The young, the old. Personal belongings, things that were once precious to the now dead people lay trampled and scattered everywhere. The Nequam didn't have much and didn't keep many possessions, but whatever they did have, they cherished and kept close to their hearts.

He wanted to cry but couldn't. The tears didn't come and he couldn't utter a sound. His throat didn't work. He choked every time he was about to say something. His family, his mother, father and little sister lay somewhere in the midst of this...whatever you wanted to call it. From the hoisted up beams and sticks, it was clear that the Men of Scelus had themselves a lot of fun. Sick and cruel tortures. Furcifer knew that he didn't want to find his family.

He turned around and looked at Prince Leo. He was kneeling on the ground crying. Shedding the tears he, Furcifer, was unable to shed. Feeling the pain he was presently unable to feel. But wasn't this his fault? Somehow, he knew that all this was his fault. First, the medicum tried to kill him but failed. Then, they burn his mansion down and he escapes and heads for the Nequam. Why? They didn't have anything to do with whatever it is that's going on. They had no part in it. This prince fellow knew he was danger, but he still headed for his people, the innocent Nequam he knew couldn't protect or defend themselves.

Furcifer ran up to Prince Leo, kicked him hard in the stomach and walked off.

Prince Leo lay on the ground buckled over, the pain in his heart more than the pain in his stomach. Tears still flowing across his face.

"Why father? Why?" he cried in a whisper. "Why this way?"

Prince Leo lay curled up on his side weeping, tormented by the scenes that had occurred the night before, all now replaying in his head as he lay there on the very ground they took place and surrounded by the bodies, the pieces. From beginning to end, he saw the whole thing. How the Men of Scelus arrived, surrounded the camp, set fire to the forest and began the slaughter as the poor people, mostly women and children tried to escape the flames. At the same time, the men from Scelus were selecting those to keep alive for the despicable, circus entertainment afterwards. Prince Leo could see the children, the terror in their eyes, not knowing what was going on or why. He could see the horror in the eyes of their parents as they realized what was going to happen to their children and how they were powerless to stop it. They had been chased and hunted down by the Men of Scelus before, but never like this. There was something driving them this time. Something possessing them beyond the fringes of their usual cruelty and animal like ferocity. There was a crazed, brutish wildness in their eyes that obscured any semblance of humanity. That night, the Men of Scelus weren't men.

"Why?"

Prince Leo asked into the air, his face glistening with his own tears and sweat from the disturbing visions he was seeing pass before his eyes.

"Why?"

Their sufferings are over. Let it be.

"It shouldn't be this way. It shouldn't be this way."

Let it be, Leo. Let it be so.

"We should have stopped it. We should have stopped this from happening. How could you have allowed this to happen?"

Let things be as they are. Had Furcifer arisen when you told him to, you both could have prevented this. This is the way of Nox, Leo. This is the way of the land that you're in.

"We still could have done something. You could have done something. You should have."

I've allowed the people of Nox to live the way they have chosen to live. Let this be, Leo. For now. We will fix all things in good time. But let this pass.

Violent sobs shook Prince Leo's body as he lay there on the ground in the valley of horrors, where so many were slaughtered and tortured and he felt as they did. Helpless.

He cried.

Leo?

"Father?"

Where is Furcifer?

"He's gone off. He shan't return."

Then I'll give you twelve of these children to take his place. Train them to guide my people across the Seven Mountains and the Seven Seas.

All of a sudden, there was a stirring in twelve different places across the charred valley. Twelve children began to gather themselves and get up off the ground, their skin and hair perfect as before. All of them younger than ten moons. Six boys and six girls. They all got up simultaneously and began to walk towards the place where Prince Leo lay.

Give them power and show them our will. Get up Leo. There is much to be done.

"Yes father," Prince Leo said, wiping his face and beginning to raise himself off the ground as the children approached him. He had to pull himself together. He had to finish his mission here. He had to make it to the end and look Casus in the eye. The muscles in his jaw tensed. He had come this far. It would all soon be over for him, while it was just now beginning for Nox. But yes, his father was right. There was much to be done.

Chapter Four

Prince Leo took the children away from that bloody place to a secluded spot on the shores of the lake Miseria. There, he taught them everything there was to teach. The poor children had remembered everything of that night. They had been forced to grow up fast. The terrible memories were ingrained in their minds and would live with them forever. Therefore, Prince Leo felt there was no reason to hold back. What they had both seen and endured had ripped their childhood away from them. Besides, more lay ahead of them. King Unus had called them and risen them for a specific purpose. He wanted, demanded something of them. It seemed too much to ask of children, but Prince Leo knew his father could not be denied.

And so he taught them. He taught them the Testament of King Unus. He showed them the path of the Standard of Light. He trained them in the ways of thought and how to access King Unus' light which lay deep down inside of them, within their Intimus Essentia. He showed them how to allow it to come forth, first through meditation, then through everyday life and living. How to be led by it in every which way. Allowing it to guide ones' walk, talk, thought, entire life. Prince Leo taught them how to live in the flow of the River Vivere although it lay far away, running its course before the gates to King Unus' private chambers within the very heart of the City of Sedes. He taught them the consciousness and very the essence of the land of Lux and its king. At the end of many, many days, Prince Leo looked over them with pride.

"Conduct. You must all remember that conduct is of great importance. If your conduct is eschewed, your consciousness will wane. And if your consciousness wanes, you will not have access to Sedes and its infinite wisdom. If you don't have access to wisdom, you will misstep. Your misstepping can and will cause your demise. But not only your demise, but the demise of others."

The children sat before him silently, digesting what he was telling them. Finally one of them spoke up.

"Someone mis-stepped didn't they?" asked Primus. "That's what caused the Men of Scelus to attack the Nequam."

Prince Leo smiled a painful smile at the boy. He had learned. He had learned well. Although Prince Leo had tried to hide it, the boy, using what he had taught them, discerned what he had tried to conceal. To the conscious mind illuminated by the light of Sedes and its wisdom, there are no secrets. Only things that will be revealed in time, in their perfect time.

Insurrectum Ex Lux Lucis

"I will not deceive you. What happened to the Nequam could have been avoided. King Unus had chosen one of your own, now lost tribe, to be of rescue. All he needed do was trust me and bring me to your people. He didn't."

Prince Leo paused and looked into their eyes. Some of them were crying silently. He could see the anger in the faces of others. Scenes of that terrible night were replaying themselves in their little minds and they were beginning to see the gravity of what they were involved in. How important everything they had been taught was. The pressure was immense but it was on their shoulders and they would have to bear it.

"The king still could have stopped it, could he not have," asked Quinta.

"Yes Quinta," Prince Leo replied honestly. "He could have. But, he chose not to. He had chosen someone to save your people and, for whatever reason, that person chose not to. King Unus allowed your people to feel the horrors of that choice. Just as now he has chosen you to save many people in Nox. And if you refuse, he may allow those people who you are to save to feel what you and your people have felt."

It hurt Prince Leo to speak like this, especially to children. He grieved deeply inside. But they knew his heart. They had been with him for many days now. He had taught them to feel a person, especially a person's pain. Now, they were feeling his. They knew he cared for them, loved them. They also knew that he didn't want them to do what they had to do. He didn't want them to fight in this rebellion but rather would take them in his arms, away to the beautiful land of Lux and have them cared for and enjoy the childhood that was so ruthlessly stolen from them. But in turn, he felt what they bore within their hearts. The overwhelming urge to do something. To avenge in whatever way they could, the destruction of their tribe, their people, their way of life, their families, their parents and siblings. They felt a deep sense of gratitude to King Unus of raising them up and giving them a chance. They wanted to make a difference. They wanted to make an impact.

"When will we begin?" asked Nonus.

"I am now going to send you away to the City of Spes were a man named Fortis is king. He, too, and most of the people in that city have felt the pain of loss and they are now loyal to King Unus. There you must wait until the noon day turns black as night and I come to you in a mist. Then you will have all the power you need to do whatever it is that you are directed from Sedes."

The children were silent.

Tertia, a child only five moons, came up to Prince Leo and put her arms around him. Then they all came and embraced him. A tear now slid down Prince Leo's face. Oh father! these are just children! His children. He, Leo, was the only father they knew now. The only one to be with them and to guide them. And he would have to leave them for a while. Alone. Just as he had left Mearor in Spes.

His children. These were his own children now. First, Primus, then Secundus. Three girls, Tertia, Quarta and Quinta. Two more boys, Sextus and Septimus. There was the gentle Octava then there was Nonus. Decima, the kind hearted girl of eight. Undecimus, a silent one. And Duodecima who

Prince Leo feared was unable to edure all that lay before her.

"Now children," Prince Leo said, pulling himself away and wiping his face. He had to be strong. "It is time for you to leave this place and find the way to the City Spes. Primus, you will lead them. And as you go, don't be afraid. I will cover you in a shroud that no one will see you as you go. You will get there safely. Primus, remember to give my regards to King Fortis. Octava, do not forget my message to the girl Mearor."

With that, the children turned to leave. Some of them drying tears that would not be dried. They loved Leo and didn't want to leave him. They wanted to stay with him by the lake forever. They wanted to embrace him forever. But alas, they could not.

Prince Leo watched them as they went, his heart breaking into a million pieces. This was all very difficult. He felt his pain slowly killing him. He felt as though, from the moment he set foot on the soil of Nox, he had been bleeding internally. Now that bleeding worsened. He was sick. He wasn't well and his strength was ebbing. The toll of everything was getting to him and his heart was suffering. He felt the pains of these people too intensely. He felt all their sorrows even more than they did. He felt the emotions of the entire land of Nox and it was beginning to get unbearable, even for him.

He slouched down on one knee and grabbed at his chest. He knelt there panting for a while before spitting out some blood that came up into his mouth. Prince Leo was dying.

THE CITY OF HAERESIS

Chapter One

Prince Leo was weary as he traveled down the road, south toward the River Mentiri. He was tired and didn't want to be in Nox anymore. This whole affair had been extremely taxing from the moment he embarked on it. The pain and suffering in this land was even more than he had thought and he felt it all very deeply. He felt the heart cries of the land and its people, it's trees, plants, animals, rocks, cliffs, valleys, mountains and sky. They all, everything, calling to him, yearning and pressing upon him for redemption. But he could do nothing but endure. Shun and turn away from the pleading, beseeching hands outstretched to him. And the pain that stung the worst was that of the children and having to turn away from them. For the meantime at least. Yet, still, his heart was losing its strength. It had been broken many, many times over since he entered the land of Nox and it was slowly giving way.

"How goes it friend?"

Prince Leo turned around to see a cheerful looking man with a pack on his back. He wasn't in the mood for the likes of him. He didn't want to look at anyone smiling and happy with all that was going on. He didn't want to talk to someone chirpy. The man was all of those and from the look of him, he too had been traveling for a long time.

"I am well, I suppose," Prince Leo replied wearily. "And you?"

"Well you suppose? Aren't you excited? Quite thrilled actually? To be so close. So near. The river is not too far off. We shall be there in no time."

Prince Leo looked at the man now walking beside him. Somewhat marveling at his exhilaration. The man caught Leo staring at him.

"My apologies," the man said with a big smile across his face as he offered his hand. "I am not quite myself. My name is Peregrinator. I'm from the City of Solitus."

"The City of Solitus," Prince Leo echoed, trying to get the geography of Nox right in his burdened mind. "Is that not far to the north?"

"Yes, indeed. Not far from the City of Dubito. To the left of it actually and a little south of the City of Artes. I've traveled all this way to finally see Prince Leo and to hear him speak for myself. I've read all his books and memorized many passages from them. Now, I shall finally see and hear him in person."

"Pardon," Prince Leo said with squinted eyes and a jumbled up mind. "Did you say Prince Leo?"

"Yes. Prince Leo of Lux. Why, isn't that why you're going to the city?

To see the prince?"

Then he remembered. The land of Nox had its own Prince Leo of Lux, or someone who claimed to be him. There was a fellow in the City of Haeresis who declared that he was Prince Leo of Lux, Son of King Unus and that he was in Nox to try to convert the people before his father came to destroy them all. Casus and Imperator Dulos had set this up a long time ago in anticipation of the arrival of the real Prince Leo. Now, so many were ensnared in this falsehood and, though it was one of the great jokes of Nox, it was also a very prevalent and powerful belief.

"Yes. Of course. To see Prince Leo of Lux," Leo replied. "Why else would I be headed for the city?"

They arrived at the banks of the River Mentiri by sunset. Peregrinator's eagerness had kept him talking incessantly the entire time. Talking about any and everything that could come to mind. Prince Leo only half listened. He wanted to rest, now more than ever. He wanted to sit down and rest. Be alone for a while. Not teaching anyone, not talking to anyone and not caring about anyone. He was tired. But there was no time for rest. Everything was on schedule and had to stay that way. The precision of the timing for all the events that had taken place and were going to take place had been accurately planned and had transpired as such. Taking time now to rest would set everything off balance. He had to keep pace. He had to stick to the plan. If he didn't, things wouldn't end up the way they were supposed to. Timing was everything. Just as he had instructed the children, one must flow with the currents of the River Vivere. Going against that flow brought chaos. Casus was a prime example. A sad example.

Except for the sound of the river, there was silence. Peregrinator had stopped talking. Prince Leo turned and looked at him. He was staring into the fog on top of the river and was as still a statue.

"Are you well?" Prince Leo asked him.

There was no response. Peregrinator remained still.

"Peregrinator."

Prince Leo reached out and grabbed him on the arm. It was as if the man had gone into a trance of some sort.

"Peregrinator. Are you well?" he asked again.

"Uh? Oh. Yes. I am...I am well," Peregrinator replied, snapping back into reality. "Friend, would you mind sitting with me? We can cross tomorrow. It would be better crossing tomorrow don't you think? We can rest here tonight. I'm quite tired and I'm sure you are too."

"Sure," Prince Leo replied. "But I was certain you were beside yourself wanting to get to the city."

"Yes, yes. But tomorrow. It will still be there."

"Well, then tomorrow it is," Prince Leo said.

They made camp by the river bank. Prince Leo busied himself gathering wood whilst Peregrinator produced some dried morsels from his pack and worked at preparing it. They soon devoured what little they had and were resting about a blazing fire, gazing into the night sky. Strangely, Peregrinator had been silent most of the time. Not that it bothered Prince Leo. He did however, know that there was something weighing very heavily on his mind. Peregrinator's mood had changed so suddenly. It was obvious that he was in deep thought and wrestling with himself. Finally, he began to speak.

"You know, in Solitus, we pride ourselves on being just ordinary people. We don't get too much into ideas or ask too many questions about why things are the way that they are. We just accept what we see. Most all my people don't care for tales of Lux or a King Unus or the existence of a Lord Casus or any of that. It's not like they believe it or disbelieve it. They just don't want to be bothered."

He paused for a bit before continuing.

"But me, I was a strange child. It had always seemed to me that there was a reason behind everything. A cause. I just always believed that there was something out there, playing a part in everything that happened. I've always wanted to know why? How come things are so. You know, the way that they are. Why? That's the question of life. Why?"

Again, brief silence before he continued.

"As a child, while most of my friends were out playing, I spent my free time reading books. Lots and lots of books. I read and studied the Numinis doctrines of man and his place, I devoured theories on primary doubt from the City of Dubito, read letters from the City of Despero, studied treatises on the Picturae belief systems, writings from the City Timidus and even got my hands on a few pamphlets from Magus. But after reading something written by Prince Leo, I...I just knew that there was something to it. There had to be. I read everything on Prince Leo, on Lux, King Unus, the Crystal City of Sedes, Casus and his insurrection. I read and reread the tales of how this land used to be different, very different from what it is now. I researched and talked to people. Do you know that this land used to be called Hortulus? Did you know that?"

"Oh really," Prince Leo replied, feigning surprise.

"Oh yes. The name meant 'little garden'. Can you imagine? A beautiful place of flowers, fruit and peace. Abundance of every good thing. Work, not labor. Strong, healthy bodies everywhere. Happy children. What a place! Very much like the land of Lux is now, far away. And Prince Leo is here to make everything right. To restore it all. That's why he's here, living among us. Imagine that! Living amongst us here in this land. He left his beautiful Sedes to live here!"

Peregrinator fell silent for a while. Actually a long while. Leo knew however, that he wasn't finished. That he was still thinking, wrestling. Fighting with himself; struggling with something in his mind. There was no need to rush him. It was going to come out in its own time. And so it did.

"Friend, tell me, have you heard of the book Inconcessus Sententa?"

Ah!

"What's the name of it?" Prince Leo asked.

"Inconcessus Sententa. It's a book that has been out of late. Strange work but masterfully done."

"I think I have heard of it," Prince Leo replied.

"It's a troubling piece. Disturbing."

"Why do you ask about it?" Prince Leo inquired.

"I came across a copy not long after I set out on my way here. I've read and reread every book that I own and so I figured I'd purchase it for my travel."

"And?" Prince Leo urged.

"I don't know. My mind. My thoughts. They're all in an awful mess."

"How is that?"

Peregrinator shifted nervously. It was obvious that he was uncomfortable.

"The abominable book has no author. No one knows who wrote it. I've inquired of everyone I've seen on the way here and no one who has read it knows. There are only rumors surrounding it. Some say that it was written by a mad man, but those who say that are those who clearly haven't read the work. Others say that there is another type of man, a strange man, here in Nox, and from Lux perhaps, who is the author. Some think that theory makes sense. They say that there has been trouble and uprisings in some of the cities and that this strange person is at the bottom of it. Others, however, will tell you that it is the true Prince Leo of Lux who penned the book. That implies that the Prince Leo that we are going to see in the City of Haeresis is an imposter. I am in a state of horrid confusion. Who is this author? Who is this person and where is he from? Where did he get his revolutionary ideas and why doesn't he show himself? Why hide when you clearly know the truth and understand all things. This man, I tell you, is a genius! Why not help inquiring minds? Why leave us to wallow in murky waters when you have the answers we need? It's not right. It's much rather a ghastly thing to do."

Prince Leo sat in silence listening to Peregrinator venting his frustration. He felt compassion. He felt the pain and confusion this man bore and carried around inside of him. He wanted to do something to relieve him of it, but he knew he couldn't. Not yet.

"All in good time, dear friend. Mysteries become clear as day in their own time. You must be patient."

"I hope the time comes soon, friend. A drowning man haven't much time for patience."

The next morning, they broke camp and found a boatman to take them across. Again, Peregrinator fell into silence. The river was black as night and its waters cool to the touch, almost icy. There was a misty fog that hung over the water, impairing sight in any which distance. It seemed impossible that any living thing could inhabit its stream. The river itself, however, acted like a living thing. Like a long, black serpent, slithering its way across the land. Soon, they were across the River Mentiri and headed for the City Haeresis.

From the bank of the river, there lay before them a well traveled road. Solid as if paved, though it had been pounded into form by human feet. The feet of many seeking inspiration and enlightenment of some sort from the Prince Leo of Haeresis, Son of King Unus. Many just like Peregrinator, who had left their friends and family to travel across the entire land of Nox, only to attain some meaning to their lives, to find the truth. Leo shuddered at the thought of it. The poor, the hungry, the sick, all making the great sacrifice.

As they approached the city, a bizarre scene unfolded before their eyes. Many people lay on the side of the road, moaning and chanting prayers. At first Leo didn't know what to make of it. But as he listened closely, he heard them pleading and entreating the pardon of their land, begging the prince to have mercy on them and their children. That they weren't even worthy to behold his face. To even be in the same city as he was. To even be alive and breathe the same air as he did. Over and over they said these things as they rolled around, turning themselves over on the ground. From the looks of many of them, they hadn't bathed for days and had been doing this for a considerable amount of time.

"Many of these people can no longer stand up straight," Peregrinator said to Leo. "Their bodies have grown accustomed to the prostrate position."

Prince Leo hardly knew what to think of it all. He had heard of this before but had never seen it. For miles, people lay on the ground, chanting, pleading, entreating, crying, and sincerely too. The sick, the crippled, the young, the old, the dying. Beautiful and ugly alike. All lay in distress. Prince Leo was overcome and couldn't help the tears that came to his eyes. He began to slump to the ground but Peregrinator held him up as they continued on their way to the city.

The walls of the city were great and one could see that from the top of its high walls, a smoke rose up into the sky. As they drew closer, they could tell that it was due to the burning of some sorts of fragrant incense. It wasn't long before the two newcomers were coughing and could barely see. All that was visible were blurs of people, all kinds, in white robes with white pointed hats on their heads, chanting and carrying about them vials of burning incense.

Leo wanted to leave. He wanted to destroy this place and never think of it again. But he was here for a reason. And beyond the smoke, the burning incense and amidst the white robes, he felt a very familiar presence. Stronger here than anywhere else in Nox.

Imperator Dulos watched him with spiteful eyes filled with hate. He watched his every move. Prince Leo of Lux, here, in his principal city. Everywhere else in Nox he had to share jurisdiction, in one way or the other, with his fellow Imperators. But here, in Haeresis, he was in complete control. Lord Casus totally surrendered the city to him. Gave him free rein. Here he was lord. Here he was king. And that's how it was going to stay. And now that he was looking at Prince Leo, he was certain, that was how it was going to stay.

The prince was tired, weak. Weakened by the stress of all he had seen. Depleted by all the pain around him. The thing about Prince Leo was that he couldn't walk among hurting people and not feel, very deeply, what they felt. He could not see pain and not feel pain. He could not hear a scream and not echo that scream within himself. He could not disconnect himself from these people, any people. His father was King of All Lands and so he was Prince of All Lands, that meant of all people. Any and every where. And that was what was killing him. The dear prince wasn't at full strength. His energy was waning with every step, every breath. Look how he moved. Look how he covered his eyes from the smoke and how his eyes watered. Look at how his leg shakes when he steps.

"Come, dear prince," Imperator Dulos whispered. "Come and bow to our prince, our very own Prince Leo of Lux."

All of a sudden, a throng gathered about them and began to sweep them forward. Peregrinator didn't know what to think of this. It was as though both he and his friend got caught up in a wave. The people pressed their bodies against them and moved them forward in a single direction, the entire time chanting and swinging their vials of burning incense. The smoke was unbearable and, overcome, both he and his companion moved in whatever direction they were urged by the mass of bodies.

It wasn't long before they came upon golden steps. There the throng stopped. Both he and his friend climbed the steps, at first to get away from the smoke that was burning and irritating their eyes. When they had climbed high enough, however, and could see a little better, they noticed that there were people in white standing on either side of the steps pointing them in the upward direction . So they continued to climb the golden staircase until, finally, they got to a platform shielded from the sun by a canopy of golden cloth hoisted upon white marble pillars.

There, at the top, some sort of court was assembled. There were children in red robes, swinging golden vials of burning incense of a different fragrance than those below. There were women dressed in white linen on their knees in the middle of the black marble floor and a wall of men on either side of the platform, in order of increasing age and also dressed in white. The men formed a column on either side all the way up to a throne upon which sat a middle aged man clad in a purple robe, a golden sash about his waist and a moderately jeweled crown upon his head. Large, burly guards stood on either side of him, holding both, a javelin in one hand and a sword of brass in another. A teenaged girl dressed in a golden gown waved a large, peacock feathered fan with a long golden handle before the man on the throne.

Peregrinator was in awe. He was overwhelmed by the splendor for the court before him and his eyes were dazzled by the beauty and grace of it all. He fell to his knees before the man he knew for certain had to be Prince Leo, Son of Unus. Whatever reservations he had once harbored now fled his mind and he now believed himself to be seeing clearly. He had only to see for himself, behold the glory of King Unus' son to reaffirm what he had to have always known to be true. He bowed his face to the floor before him in worship and adoration..

He heard a noise, a rustling. He knew something was going on around him but he didn't raise his head or look up. He didn't want anything to interrupt this moment, so delicate, so sublime. He wanted to stay here and be here this way forever. Oh, if only he could stay in the court of Prince Leo! Surely, then his life would be fulfilled.

He felt gentle but firm hands grab hold of his shoulders, pulling him to his knees. As he looked up, he realized that it was the prince himself. He had come down from his throne and was touching him.

"Welcome, friend, to the City of Haeresis. I am Prince Leo of Lux, Son of King Unus. What is your name?"

The prince was actually talking to him. To him! He couldn't find the words to say. He desperately wanted to speak but was unable to. All he could do was cry. And so he did.

"No need for tears friend," the man said smiling at him. "All tears will be wiped away."

The prince began wiping away his tears. Peregrinator didn't know what to do. He couldn't believe that this was actually happening. The prince was everything he had thought he would be. Kind, friendly and warm. Yes. This was his prince. The wielder of all truth.

"And who is your companion," the prince said looking at his friend who had traveled with him, standing on the side.

"Friend, tell us your name. Unless, of course, you too are unable to speak."

There were slight giggles in the crowd gathered upon the platform.

"I," his friend began to speak, feet firmly planted and standing upright with his back straight, "am Prince Leo of Lux, the one and true Son of King Unus of Lux, Master and Lord of All Lands."

Chapter Two

Peregrinator spun around on his knees, his surprise obvious. What was it that he just heard him say? Did that fellow who had been traveling with him on the road just say that he was Prince Leo?

There were murmurs all over the platform and it was clear that the prince himself was in shock. After taking a moment to recover himself, he cleared his throat and spoke again, calmly.

"Then, by all means, please tell us, who am I?"

"I can definitely tell you who you are not. You are not the Son of King Unus."

The murmurs of surprise in no time turned into growls of anger and fire blazed in the eyes of the men lining the sides of the throne.

"Beware stranger," the prince spoke almost in a whisper but with authority, "we don't take kindly to heresy in this city. All indecent and improper behavior is checked at the gates."

"Nonetheless, I speak nothing but the truth."

Peregrinator was horrified. What sort of madness was this? Why was this fellow doing this? What was wrong with him? Could it be that he had inhaled too much incense coming into the city? Could that be the cause of his lunacy?

The prince, it was obvious, was vividly annoyed with this imposter. He began to back away and proceeded to take his seat on the throne. He sat and then stared at the man who called himself Unus' true son.

"I will have you know that you are not the first to come into our city making these claims," the prince addressed the stranger. "And you most likely, won't be the last. We have dealt with those before you, as we are going to deal with you and will continue to deal with those after you."

The prince snapped his fingers and immediately two guards came up the stairs and grabbed the man. Peregrinator didn't know what to think. He had traveled with this man and he had showed no signs of insanity. Why here? Why now? The prince began to speak.

"You will be whipped at the bottom of these very steps by day and imprisoned in the dungeon by night. This will happen everyday until you recant by day before these steps the heresy you have uttered here today."

Then he ordered the guards to take him away and Peregrinator saw his friend dragged off to be flogged.

Peregrinator didn't know what to think of the whole affair. He felt very uncomfortable with the whole thing. It had been days since his friend had been sentenced to daily floggings in public view before the Solium ex Leo, the golden steps leading up to the throne of the prince. And sure enough, every day his friend was flogged before the people who cursed and spat at him. He could not stand the sight of it. He avoided the place. He couldn't bear the thought of his former companion resting his eyes upon him. He felt like a traitor.

But why should he feel this way? What wrong had he done? It wasn't his fault. The man all of a sudden fell mad and began speaking lunacies. Making impossible claims. What happened to him was natural. What did he expect? To walk into the City of Haeresis, declare himself prince and straightway be deposited on the throne? He knew the risks of what he did and he took those risks. Wasn't it natural that he bear the consequences of the risks he took?

If indeed everything was so simple, why was he feeling this intolerable weight in his chest, constraining him and weighing upon him? Wretched, cursed affair! The whole thing was. He had nothing to do with it, yet he felt as though he was in the thick of the matter. By now, he was dressed in a white robe and given a vial of burning incense. He had become one of those they had encountered in the streets the first day they arrived in the city. With his white robe, hat and vial of incense, he blended in perfectly. One couldn't tell him from another person. But the nagging in his soul would yet drive him mad. Everything would have been fine had he had no companion traveling with him into the city. Had he been alone and met the prince the way he did, every doubt, every suspicion he had harbored would have vanished from his mind like a dead leaf falls off a tree. He would have been free to give himself up wholeheartedly and without reservation. He would have been free to listen intently to the prince when he came down the steps daily to teach the people. He would have been enthralled and mesmerized like everyone else. But now, stinging questions seized upon him like wild dogs, slowly tearing him down. He clutched ever firmly under his white robe, his copy of Inconcessus Sententa.

That evening, when the sun had cooled its venom and there began to settle a gentle evening breeze upon the city, Leo was taken down from the whipping post before the steps. The contraption was designed so that he hung from above by his two hands. This gave the men with the whips his entire body to lash all day and for as long as they pleased. They often allowed anyone who wished to have a go at teaching the heretic a lesson to whip him a few lashes, all the while urging him to recant. He was, however, taken down every evening before the prince came down in the cool evening. He was taken and chained in the dungeon to wait for the following day when the whole thing would be repeated.

Tonight though, Leo would have a visitor. Imperator Dulos had been watching him intently and decided to himself that he ought to go pay his respects, perhaps even apologize for the cruel hospitality. And so he waited, waited for the scared Hour of the Imperators, the dead of night.

Prince Leo sat with his back facing the wall of the dungeon though barely touching it. The whips that burned into his flesh daily made resting intolerable. He was unable to sleep at night, because it entailed lying down on some surface which only caused exceptionable agony and reopened wounds, wounds that couldn't heal because as they began to mend through the night, they were whipped open during the day. The only time he was able to get any sleep was when he hung from the whipping pole, in between the lashings. The only reason he could now bear to sit was because he had been standing since he was brought in that evening and his feet were tired. So he braced himself for the pain and sat, in torment. He sat with his head bent down, resting on his chest. Whatever blood he had left slowly seeping onto the floor around him from the wounds that were reopening due to the slight movement and his sitting down.

Imperator Dulos appeared out of the shadows of the dungeon, slithering out of its darkness.

"Ah, my dear prince," Imperator Dulos spoke and with no small amount of sarcasm. "It breaks my heart to see you this way. Oh! How terrible."

Prince Leo neither moved nor acknowledged he was there.

"Can't these wretched fools tell who you are? How very uncivilized! They ought to be punished don't you think? What shall I do to them, my lord? What would suit you? Tell me, and I'll have it done at once."

No response. No movement.

"Thinking? Well, I've got an idea, why don't I get Imperator Homicida to give them the same fate he and Imperator Pravus gave the Nequam? That ought to teach these filth to treat the Lord of Sedes this shameful, contemptuous way! What do you say?"

Still no response.

"Not talking, my lord?" asked Imperator Dulos, bending down to Prince

Leo. "Has your humble servant found displeasure in your eyes?"

Silence.

"Look at you," Imperator Dulos said, straightening up, his voice now filled with contempt. "You are nothing Prince Leo of Lux. Do you hear me? Nothing! You shouldn't have come here. You should have stayed with daddy, were it is safe. Who's going to protect you now my lord? Look at you, being whipped every day by these...these...maggots!

"What, did you think? That you were going to come here and change everything? Have us all under your thumb like before. No!" Imperator Dulos screamed. "No! Never! I hate you and I hate your despicable father! I hate everything you all stand for. I hate you!"

Imperator Dulos was losing control of himself as tears were filling the brim of his eyes. Prince Leo still hadn't moved neither acknowledged that he was there. The tears began to fall down Imperator Dulos' face and he hastily tried to wipe them away.

"I'm not even going to wait for Lord Casus to kill you," Imperator Dulos said in a whisper, desperately trying to regain composure. "I'm going to kill you myself."

Imperator Dulos raised his right hand and his already long sharp fingernails began to grow until they looked like long knives.

"I am going to cut your heart out, Prince Leo, and send it to Lord Casus in a little golden box as a gift. Maybe he might send it to your precious daddy as his gift to the great and mighty King Unus, Master of All Lands. How will your father like that?"

Imperator began to bend over Prince Leo and as he began to draw his hand back to thrust his deadly fingernails into the chest of Leo, two sharp blades pointed under his chin and into his throat. Slowly and gently, he stepped back and moved away from Prince Leo. There, standing on either side of Prince Leo, stood Truculentus and Tonitrus, two of Sedes' mightiest warriors with their swords pointing directly into the walls of his throat. Imperator Dulos knew hate when he saw it and there was much too much of it in their eyes. He knew they would not hesitate whatsoever and that their skill with those swords was beyond mention. Trembling and frightfully afraid to utter another word, he retreated into the darkness of the shadows and disappeared.

Prince Leo neither moved the entire time nor uttered a single word.

Chapter Three

Peregrinator, in his white robe and hat and swinging his vial of burning incense, mixed into the crowd of people that morning and tried his hardest not to look in the direction of the man being whipped at the foot of the golden steps. But he heard the sound of the lash, nonetheless, against the flesh that had by now become as calloused as the ground he was standing on. Though there were a million other noises around him, he could only hear one sound. The unfurling whip against now leathery skin. The man being whipped made no sound. He didn't scream out nor did he beg for mercy. Peregrinator couldn't help but think how much of a lesser man he was. By now he would have been recanting everything he had said since the day he was born. To endure such dreadful tortures must be quite inhuman. How could one, why would one....

"Aaaaiiieeeee!!"

Peregrinator turned around, half startled out of his wits. The vial of burning incense in his hand fell to the ground spewing ashes and producing a small explosion of smoke.

"T'was not a dream! T'was not a dream! Oh! Oh! Mercy! Mercy!"

An old man, an arm's breadth away from Peregrinator, was beside himself and going quite out of his mind. He was experiencing a fit of some kind, but running backwards with his eyes transfixed on the man being whipped, Peregrinator's old traveling companion.

"He's real!! He's real! Oh! Oh!" the old man was screaming at the top of his lungs.

He was running backward so fast the poor man tripped on the helm of his own robe and fell over. By now, guards were beginning to approach him as the scene was becoming distracting to the worshipers. Peregrinator rushed over to the old man to try to quiet him and, also, because he was curious.

"Old man. Calm down. Calm down," Peregrinator coaxed.

"No! No! It's him! It's him! He's real! I thought he was a dream! But he's real!"

The old man was terrified. Tears were running down his face and he was completely beside himself with fright. Peregrinator looked around and saw that the guards were gaining on them. If the guards took the old man away, he might never get a chance to find out what exactly it was that he was talking about. He picked up the crazed man in his arms, kicking and screaming, and took him a good distance away. The guards, seeing him being carried off and his shrieks drowned out by the distance, turned around and gave up the pursuit.

"Oh! Oh! He's real! It all happened! It all really happened! Oh!"

When they were finally at a safe enough distance that the old man's screaming was of no consequence, Peregrinator found an alley and put him down gently.

"Shhh!" Peregrinator commanded. "Or the guards will come and take you away. Who knows what they'll do to you."

"He's real," the old man said, spittle across his face, but finally beginning to settle down. "It all wasn't a dream."

"What are you talking about?" Peregrinator asked.

The old man suddenly grabbed Peregrinator by the shoulders in a grip of steel. His eyes became enlarged and his countenance became as someone possessed.

"That man!"

"The one being whipped?" Peregrinator asked.

"Whipped? Oh! Oh! We are all dead men. We are all dead men."

Peregrinator was confused. He didn't know what was going on and what he was hearing wasn't making any sense.

"Do you know him? Have you seen him before?" Peregrinator asked desperately seeking information.

"We thought it was a dream." The man said, loosening his grip on Peregrinator's shoulders. "We thought it couldn't be real. It didn't make sense."

The old man appeared to be returning to his senses. A notion which gave

Peregrinator some hope.

"What happened?"

The old man's eyes glazed over and he seemed to go into a trance as he spoke.

"I am from the City of Dubito. I am a foreman at the Lingua Printing Press. Have been for a long time. I went to bed one night as I usually do, early, so that I could be at work on time the next morning. But when I woke up that morning, I woke up to the worst horror imaginable."

"What do you mean? What happened?" pressed Peregrinator.

"I was swimming. Swimming for my life."

Swimming?!

"There was a flood?" Peregrinator asked.

"Yes and no . I haven't the slightest idea."

"Old man, you aren't making any sense."

The old man snapped out of his trance and looked directly into his eyes.

"Of course I'm not making sense. The whole thing didn't make sense. I was swimming. I was swimming in water...in ice... in sand...in fire...clouds maybe, who knows, and all at once."

"What?!"

"Yes. What?! And that man did it. That man. The entire city was flooded with the ghastly stuff that burned the flesh, froze the flesh, sanded the flesh all at once. That man. He stood atop the Lingua Building watching it all. Watching the city in terror. Watching us all suffering. I saw him. The entire city saw him. We all knew he was doing it, whatever it was. I saw him call to a carpenter from the city, a man I have had mend many a chair for me. He called to the man and the man flew up in the air to him. They spoke and it seemed as if the carpenter vanished. Soon, we all fell asleep. When we awoke, we were all out of our homes and out in the streets were we had been wasting away in the unnatural substance. All of us but the man and the carpenter."

Peregrinator's mind was at a stand still. He couldn't process what he had just heard. He was having difficulty. The man slowly continued.

"We thought it was a dream. It had to be a dream. Nothing like that is possible. Ever. Some had doubts and few even believed that it had actually happened. But most of us believed it was a dream and tried to forget. I couldn't though. How can you? Especially with the carpenter really gone, his home and shop abandoned. Some people said that there are tales of a strange man in Nox, others say its this Prince Leo fellow. I tried to forget, but I hardly sleep nights. I've read books, I've talked to people, I've questioned people and all I get are tales. So finally, I decided to at least come down here to see if anything might connect."

Peregrinator was still having problems comprehending all that he had heard. He was trying to see how it all fit or even followed some form of logic.

"Whipped!" the old man suddenly said with a start. "You people are mad! I must get as far away from this place as soon as possible! You will all die!"

The old man struggled to his feet and fled. Peregrinator sat on the ground, with his eyes glazed over, holding his troubled head in his hands.

That evening, as was usual, Leo was brought down from the whipping pole. The sun was setting and the prince was going to teach the people. Two guards began to drag the corpse of a body toward the dungeon. The rest of the city was pretty much deserted due to the fact that everyone was gathering at the Solium ex Leo, the foot of the golden stairs to listen to the prince teach and give them words of wisdom, the keys and secrets to life. Even the guards were in a hurry to lock up their prisoner and hopefully return to grab some of the golden nuggets that the prince might spew from his mouth. Therefore, they were completely taken by surprise, when, at the gate to the dungeon, they were attacked by one of their own people. The wild man, dressed in a white gown, hit one of them over the head from behind with a club, knocking the guard unconscious on the spot. The other guard however reacted quickly enough to escape the arch of the second swing. He was in the process of drawing his sword when a kick to the back of his left knee brought his knee crashing into the cobblestone street. That was more than enough time for the man with the club hit him hard across the face as the two escaped, one of them, his prisoner.

The two ran as fast as they could but the noises behind them made it all too clear that they were being pursued.

"Follow me, I've read everything put into print about this city and it's prince," Peregrinator panted. "I know this city like the back of my hand."

They meandered through buildings and homes, taking alleys and back ways. Still their pursuers remained hot on their trail. No matter how perplexing the route they took, there was always someone close. Finally, Peregrinator led them into a home, kicking down the front door as they burst in. Being that everyone was at the base of the Solium ex Leo, yearning inspiration, no one was home. Up the stairs and into the bedroom, slamming the window shutters open, Peregrinator turned to Prince Leo.

"This house is built onto the city walls. Jump out and we'll be outside. There's a moat at the bottom. You go first."

Prince Leo sprang through the window amid a hail of arrows from up above, atop the city's walls. He, however, splashed safely into the cool waters below and instantly began to swim across. He heard a similar splash shortly afterwards, Peregrinator not being far behind. In no time, Prince Leo was across and out of the water. He glanced back as he was about to dash off and saw Peregrinator struggling, the water around him swirling red as the shower of arrows continued to descend. Prince Leo jumped back into the moat and pulled Peregrinator to land. An arrow had pierced him through his back and came out in the middle of his chest.

"Go. Leave me," Peregrinator said between long, labored breaths.

"I can carry you...."

"No. No," Peregrinator interrupted him, smiling. "Go. Just tell me one thing."

"What is it?"

"You wrote the book."

"Yes," Prince Leo said. "I wrote the book."

Pereginator smiled. He was fading fast.

"Go. Go now. Quickly."

Still arrows continued to whiz at them.

"Please," Peregrinator pleaded. "Go. Save Nox," he said with his last breath, choking on his own blood.

Prince Leo left him lying on his side and headed for the River Mentiri.

THE FORTRESS OF VORAGO

Prince Leo stumbled and fumbled his way, half crawling amongst the brush and trees until he got to the River Mentiri. At the banks of the river, he finally collapsed. Fatigue and hunger impaled him and it seemed as though he had lost all strength. Yet, there were pursuers on horseback in search of him. Lying there on the banks of the river and using his arms, he crawled his way into the dark, icy waters and its misty fog. The guards at that very instant arrived at the banks of the river and proceeded to dismount when something very strange began to happen. The river, with Prince Leo in it, began to reverse its flow. Instead of flowing downward toward the City of Haeresis, the river began to flow upward, bearing their prisoner way.

Half of the men where so horrified that they turned their horses around and began to gallop full speed, as far away from the possessed river as possible and back toward the city, screaming in panic. Others who were more audacious, decided to gallop alongside the river bank in order to try to catch up with the body in the water. But soon their horses lagged further and further behind until they gave up the chase.

By then, Prince Leo had lost consciousness.

When he regained consciousness, he lay on the bank of the river, in a forest. His body ached and his head was pounding. His back felt like leather stretched beyond its capacity and his skin was stiff. He struggled to his feet, however, and stood.

As he stood on his feet, he began to sway and almost fell backwards into the river. His head was killing him. It felt as though someone had a knife in it and was turning the blade every which way. But he tried to focus and steady himself. He took one step forward, slowly. Balanced. Then took another step. Swayed a bit, but then balanced.

He looked around. How was he going to make it? Where was he? He had made the river reverse its flow in order to get away from the guards. But also, he knew that the river flowed down from Vorago, the Fortress of Casus and the surrounding Mountains and Forests of Fallacia. So then, he must be in that forest, the Forests of Fallacia. How was he going to make it through the forests and over the mountains? He hadn't the strength.

Just then, he saw coming out of the forest, his children. The remnant of the Nequam. He saw Tertia running up to him. The dear child. He was happy to see her. But what were they doing here? Weren't they supposed to be almost in the City of Spes by now. Nevertheless, he reached out to embrace her but felt, instead, a hard, solid kick crush deep into his chest. The impact was so powerful that it sent him high up into the air and backwards into the water with a pretty big splash. Blood spewed forth out of his mouth. Before his mind could shut down on him again, he looked up out of the river to see what had happened. It wasn't the children standing on the riverbank. There looking down at him, sat four of the Imperators on horseback. Around them, and as far back as he could see in the shadow of trees, were many of the other defectors from Lux who had joined them and Casus in their attempt to overthrow King Unus. Imperator Odium, however, was standing where Prince Leo had thought he saw the child. Imperator Odium being the one who had kicked him. But then everything got blurry and Prince Leo faded out.

Icy, cold water stabbed at his bare back as he lay on his stomach on the blue marble floor.

"I am uncertain, dear prince, as to whether it is proper to sleep in the presence of your host."

Prince Leo knew the voice, hated the voice. And it belonged to one person only.

"How very kind of you, Prince Leo, Son of King Unus, Lord of Sedes, to lie prostrate before me, humble Casus. You honor me too much I fear."

Prince Leo could hear the laughter around him. He tried to get up but his body would not respond. His arms were trembling in the effort but weren't quite making it.

"I do think our honored guest is trying to get up."

More laughter.

"What's the matter with those strong arms of yours? Those arms that

King Unus depends on? Can't they raise you up from sniveling on the floor like a rat!" Lord Casus screamed down at Prince Leo.

Slowly, but steadfastly, Prince Leo labored to his feet, lifted his head and looked into the face of Lord Casus of Nox. Casus was seated upon a great throne of gold adorned with rubies, sapphires, emeralds and all sorts of precious stones. He had on a scarlet red robe with a heavy golden belt about his waist, his black boots resting upon a golden footstool.

"Now. That's better," Casus said. "So tell me, what do you think of the land of Nox so far? Do you like it? It took a little while to get these people where we wanted them to be, but in time, they came around to our way of thinking?"

Prince Leo looked slowly around him. All the Imperators sat on thrones in a semi-circle around him facing Lord Casus. Imperator Metus, however, sat closest to Casus, glaring at he, Leo. The room was lavish, but dark and lighted only by a great torch directly behind Casus' throne.

"Oh, my apologies your majesty, you don't answer questions?" Lord Casus again mocked at Prince Leo, as laughter again resounded in the room.

"You disgust me," Casus said to Prince Leo.

"When do we kill him," asked Imperator Homicida.

"Do it now if you wish. I'm beginning to get ill from the stench of him. I personally don't even want to touch him," Lord Casus said waving his hand flippantly toward Prince Leo and returning to take his seat on his throne.

Imperator Homicida drew his sword, and getting up from his own throne directly behind Prince Leo, ran up behind him. Prince Leo didn't turn to face him neither did he attempt to dodge what he knew was coming. The blade passed clean through his stomach as all the other Imperators drew their swords and joined in the fray, slashing, cutting and piercing. When they had had their full, Prince Leo lay on the floor in a bloody heap, slightly convulsing, blood pouring from his mouth.

"Step away!" Lord Casus commanded them, stepping down from his throne. "I want to see him take his last breath."

The Imperators with their bloody swords, cleared away and Casus bent over and raised Prince Leo's face to his. He looked into his eyes and watched in silence the life slowly leave them. He hadn't known what exactly he had expected to see, but he was drawn into the closing eyes. Like some part of him was irresistibly pulled into that lifeless place and shut up there. Slowly, he put the head back down on the messy floor, rose to his feet and stood over the body in silence.

Epilogue

The next noon day, all over the land of Nox, suddenly began to darken. It was as if the sun began a retreat from the land, choosing to shine it's light elsewhere. An eerie feeling gripped all the people and many of them began to feel a deep sorrow welling up in the very depth of their souls, though they knew not why. As the black darkness covered the land so that one could hardly see, a white mist began to flow across Nox like a blanket. From the Fortress of Vorago, spreading out over the entire land, the mist covered and seemed to seep into every mountain, every hill, every valley, every city, every building, every home, every forest, every cave, every plant, animal and person. And then as slowly and gently as it came, it vanished and was gone. The sun, seemingly with much trepidation, gradually and grudgingly retook its place over the land of Nox.

Frederick De Leon

Insurrectum Ex Lux Lucis

Glossary of Names and Places

Acerbus dark (Acerbus Square)

Alumno student

Ars art, skill

Artes fine art (City of Artes)

Artificum Niger black art

Avidas greed (Imperator Avidas)

Caecus blind

Caputolium capitol

Casus fall (Lord Casus)

Frederick De Leon

Casta pure

Coma rays of light

Corruptela seduction (Lady Corruptela)

Corona crown

Decimus tenth

Decus pride (Imperator Decus)

Demissus dejected (City of Demissus)

Despero despair (City of Despero)

Docere enlighten

Dolor pain

Dubito doubt (City of Dubito)

Dulos deceit (Imperator Dulos)

Duodecima twelveth

Egenus destitue (City of Egenus)

Elatus haughty (City of Elatus)

Fallacia deception (Mountains and Forests of Fallacia)

Fertilis fruitful

Fletus weep

Fortis strong

Furcifer scoundrel

Homicida murderer (Imperator Homicida)

Hortulus little garden

Imperator general

Impietas unbelief

Inconcessus Sententa Forbidden Thoughts

Insulsus silly

Intimus Essentia Innermost Essence

Invidere envy

Leo lion (Prince Leo)

Lingua tongue (Lingua Printing Press)

Lux light

Magistrae teacher

Magus magic (City of Magus)

Mearor sorrowful

Medicus practitioner (medicum, pl.)

Mentiri lies (River Mentiri)

Mercator merchant

Metus fear (Imperator Metus)

Miseria distress (Lake Miseria)

Frederick De Leon
Mitis gentle

Nequam worthless (Tribe of the Nequam)

Nonus nineth

Nox night

Numinis deity (City of Numinis; Numinis Doctrines)

Octava eight

Odium hate (Imperator Odium)

Otium peace (Canyon of Otium)

Peregrinator pilgrim

Picturae picture (Picturae Faith of Artes)

Pinacothecae picture gallery

Praeco herald

Pravus immoral (Imperator Pravus)

Primus first

Procer noble

Promptus resolute

Pullus blackish, sad (River Pullus)

Quarta fourth

Quinta fifth

Radix root

Refectorium ex Astrum Hall of the Star

Scelus wickedness (City of Scelus; Men of Scelus)

Secundus second

Sedes seat (City of Sedes)

Septimus seventh

Sextus sixth

Solitus normal, ordinary (City of Solitus)

Solium throne (Solium ex Leo)

Taedi disgust (River Taedi)

Tertia third

Timidus fearful (City of Timidus)

Tonitrus thunder

Truculentus ferocious

Turbatus confused

Umbra shade (Mansion Umbra)

Undecimus tenth

Unus one (King Unus)

Frederick De Leon

Vates seer

Veneficus witch

Villicus steward

Visus sight (City of Visus)

Vitiosus morally corrupt (City of Vitiosus)

Vivere life (River Vivere)

Voluntas sense

Vorago pit (Fortress of Vorago)

About the Author

Frederick de Leon was first published at the age of seventeen when his short story "Life from Death" won him acclaim form the River Valley Student writer's Conference. Since then, he's completed two prior books, Just A Man and Eavesdropping. He is the author of over one hundred and fifty poems and twenty-five short stories. Poems of his have been featured in anthologies From the Mountaintop, Time after Time and Bending Light to name a few. In the year 2001, the International Library of Poetry featured one of his poems on their audio recording of collected works entitled *"The Sound of Poetry"* and bestowed on him both that year and the next, two Poet of Merit Awards "…for outstanding contribution to the art of poetry." He also received in the fall of 2001, a Poet of the Year Medallion and a Prometheus Muse of Fire trophy from the Famous Poet's Society.

Printed in the United Kingdom
by Lightning Source UK Ltd.
114671UKS00001B/103